Further Modern Scottish Stories

Also Edited by Robert Millar and J. T. Low
Ten Modern Scottish Stories
Five Scottish One-Act Plays

Edited by Robert Millar
Here Lies
Tensions
(Secondary English Programme)

By Robert Millar and I. S. Currie
The Language of Poetry
The Language of Prose

By Robert Millar and T. M. Brown
Put It in Writing

Further Modern Scottish Stories

Selected with an Introduction, Talking Points, and an Appendix on Making a Short Story

by

ROBERT MILLAR, M.A.,
formerly Director of the Centre for Information on the Teaching of English, Edinburgh

and

J. T. LOW, B.A., M.Litt., Ph.D.,
Moray House College of Education, Edinburgh,
Visiting Professor, Department of English,
Dalhousie University, Halifax, N.S., Canada

HEINEMANN EDUCATIONAL BOOKS
LONDON AND EDINBURGH

Heinemann Educational Books Ltd
22 Bedford Square, London WC1B 3HH

LONDON EDINBURGH MELBOURNE AUCKLAND
HONG KONG SINGAPORE KUALA LUMPUR NEW DELHI
IBADAN NAIROBI JOHANNESBURG KINGSTON
EXETER (NH) PORT OF SPAIN

ISBN 0 435 13540 6

First published 1976
Reprinted 1979

Filmset in 10/12 Garamond
by Spectrum Typesetting, London
Printed and bound in Great Britain
by Morrison & Gibb Ltd, London and Edinburgh

Contents

Introduction

We offered *Five Scottish One-Act Plays* and *Ten Modern Scottish Stories* in the belief that Scottish teachers should be given easy access to Scottish texts, should they wish to use them. The warm welcome given to these two books has encouraged us to compile the present volume of stories, this time specially chosen to appeal to the younger secondary-school reader, although the stories are capable of engaging the interest and exercising the critical talents of more mature pupils.

The stories selected present the human situation in a variety of moods—sympathetic, tragic, ironic, comic, boisterous, reflective; and it is hoped a reading of these tales may lead to an appreciation of the quality of life as lived and experienced in different Scottish settings. Geographically, the range is from Orkney and the highland north-west, through central Scotland, to the industrial belt of the lowlands; but the exact location cannot always be traced although it may be inferred from the context. The universality of the stories should ensure a wide appeal; their linguistic and technical variety should attract readers of different tastes and may encourage young students themselves to experiment with a range of styles; the Scottish flavour should add an overall piquancy and unity of tone.

A theme that runs through most of these stories is that of the individual—often a young person inexperienced and adolescent—caught in some kind of conflict within society, in the family, or within himself. Alexander Reid in *A Warm Golden Brown* shows how childhood problems may be complicated by the colour bar imposed by adults. Eona Macnicol in *The Small Herdsman* implies that life is harsher for adolescents in an urban environment than in a rural setting; and Clifford Hanley in *School Dance* illustrates the double problem of an adolescent trying to come to terms with other members of his family while trying also to resolve conflicts within himself.

Two other stories in this volume are concerned with the problem—and the loneliness—of normal adolescents within their family groups. Fred Urquhart in *Alicky's Watch* surrounds his study of an isolated but absorbed youngster with a sharp satirical portrait of a selfishly preoccupied family group in mourning. Here the tragedy of the mother's death is toned down by being set alongside the human comedy and the mock tragedy of the break-down of the watch. J. F. Hendry's *The Disinherited* uses a comic and dramatic technique to illustrate the plight of a youngster torn between loyalty to an unsympathetic family and passion for a sport. Although the method here is comic the portrayal of the isolation develops a certain pathos. These two stories have lowland or urban settings. In a third story, Edward Scouller's *Murdoch's Bull,* set in the highlands, the central character is a sub-normal adolescent who yet has confidence in his way of life because of his love for and skill in handling a difficult and dangerous animal. The tragedy here lies in the inability of the normal people of the community to understand this attachment and the value of the boy's skill; and the tragic action occurs when the life-line—the association between animal and boy—is cut.

Two of the stories make their commentary on human suffering by skirting the tragical and showing the effect of an unexpected happy ending—reprieve or survival—on character and social pattern. Iain Crichton Smith's *The Telegram* builds up tension for two mothers as they watch the bearer of a war-time telegram approach their houses. Tragedy seems inevitable for first one then the other; but by an ironical twist the tragedy by-passes them and moves to the elder—the bearer of the telegram himself. Naomi Mitchison in *On An Island* similarly seems to be building up to inevitable tragedy with all the power of imaginative anticipation; but the critical moment brings the young wife news of her husband's recovery not of his death.

There is a sombre note near the end of George Mackay Brown's *The Ferryman*, but there too tragedy hovers on the edge of the story: the emphasis remains on the varied pageantry of island life, the theme of injustice, and the wild and grim setting of the northern sea. The Scottish setting is gentler and more soothing in Eona Macnicol's story *The Small Herdsman*; and here with the switch from idyllic to sordid there also comes a transfer of feeling, of a load of sorrow, from central character to narrator, from the person who suffered to the girl who was at first merely inquisitive but who eventually becomes the sufferer. We are reminded of the transfer of sorrow from mariner to wedding guest in Coleridge's poem. There is an example of the use of this kind of device in John Thomas Low's *Jemima*, but it is here presented in a comic vein. In this story the character-narrator, unsympathetic to begin with towards Dave's enthusiasm for the bike, takes over near the end the feeling for the motorbike as living creature that Dave had built up and then suddenly discarded. *Jemima* also illustrates the importance of the natural setting in a Scottish story, its magnificence and its violence, a setting that can both inspire and terrify. In this story, too, the device of anti-climax is used in the coda. After skirting or flirting with the supernatural the author returns us to the earthy and the natural. The strange appearance of Jemima high up on the path appears after all to have a normal explanation.

Dave in *Jemima*, like the central characters in the other stories, is someone larger than life, someone who does not fit in to the social or group pattern. This is a variant of the theme we mentioned earlier as running through the selection. It is not only the adolescent who is to be sympathized with or admired or presented as a suffering being: it is the character who dares to be different and show something of the vitality of life who can give shape and pace to a story.

In the matter of structure and technique the stories tend to conform to a pattern. Most depend for their effect on a build-up to a climax, a turning-point, a moment of self-realization, which generally comes at or near the end; but most also have a coda or tailpiece that comments, explains, illuminates, or, in the case of the George Mackay Brown, Clifford Hanley, J. F. Hendry stories, breaks off on a deliberately undramatic note. The power is often felt to be in the method of narration. The reader tends to become involved in these stories because they are told from within—either by a narrator who takes part or by an author who tends to identify himself with the characters or the community. Stories that exploit a character-narrator tend to achieve the warmest tone and the closest weave—*The Ferryman, The Small Herdsman, Jemima*. Perhaps the coolest, most objective tales are Iain Crichton Smith's *The Telegram* and Alexander Reid's *A Warm Golden Brown*. In these the skill lies more in letting the situation develop and generate its own commentary and warmth.

The language tends to be informal and direct, although there are traces of a more mannered style used deliberately, for example, by Clifford Hanley in the passages of 'learned' repartee in *School Dance*, by J. F. Hendry in the opening to *The Disinherited*, and at times also by Fred Urquhart in *Alicky's Watch*. John Thomas Low in *Jemima* tends to use an exuberant exaggerated style for comic and mock heroic effect. On the other hand, the two highland stories *On An Island* and *Murdoch's Bull* are perhaps the most successful in achieving a combination of flexibility and idiomatic flavour within a quieter style. Unobtrusive touches of poetry come from George Mackay Brown in *The Ferryman*, as is to be expected; and perhaps the barest style paradoxically comes from another poet, Iain Crichton Smith, in *The Telegram* where there is a quality of classical restraint.

Our **Talking Points** may help readers to sort out their ideas about characterization, themes, technique, and social commentaries within the stories. They are also designed to bring out something of the shape and pattern. The editors hope that readers will be encouraged by these comments and questions to study the stories seriously as contributions to a literary form that seems to be flourishing in Scotland as in other parts of the world.

R.M.
J.T.L.

Note on Scottish Words

The language in which these stories are written is on the whole straightforward English, although often it has a Scottish flavour—lowland or highland. Any special Scottish words that occur will be familiar to most people. There are not many of these, but glossaries have been provided where necessary to remind readers of standard English equivalents.

Alexander Reid

A WARM GOLDEN BROWN

The brown girl from number eleven darted across Finchley Row and standing on tiptoe looked over the hedge of number ten.

'What you making, Ben?' she asked.

'Harbour,' answered Ben in a muffled voice and without looking up from the tiny artificial pool by the side of which he was sprawling on his stomach.

'Can I come and look?' she asked.

Ben sat up, blinking into the sun, glanced round quickly at the windows overlooking the garden, then nodded.

'You can if you like,' he said condescendingly. 'But only for a minute. You've got to go away as soon as you've seen it.'

The brown girl did not answer but ran round to the gate, opened it, sprang lightly over a bed of marigolds and was at his side, bent over the pond, narrow brown hands cupped over her kneecaps.

'It's a good harbour,' she said admiringly. 'It's like the one at Seaton.'

Ben squinted critically at his work. 'It's better really.' Then he added honestly, 'Of course it's not quite so big. When I'm older I'll build a real one.' He flung another glance at the windows. 'You'd better go now, Daisy,' he said uneasily. 'Mum's having a bath but if she comes through and sees us I'll catch it for letting you in.'

The brown girl pouted. A frown darkened the warm golden brown of her brow, and she flung back her bob of coal-black hair petulantly as she straightened herself.

'Why can't I play with you?' she asked a little querulously. 'I'd like to build a harbour too.'

'Girls can't build harbours.' Ben was scornful.

'I could help,' said the brown girl humbly. 'I could carry stones for you. I'll get you some from our garden if you like and then you'll be able to build a breakwater too.'

Ben's blue eyes sparkled—seeing it.

'That's an idea!' he cried enthusiastically. 'We could run it out here, below the harbour, and build a lighthouse at the end, and . . . ' He stopped suddenly and his head turned towards the window. 'I thought I heard her,' he said.

The brown girl ignored the interruption.

'Will I get the stones?' she asked eagerly, poised to turn. 'We've got heaps. Dad dug them up when he was making the shelter.'

But Ben's face had clouded. He paddled a finger in the water and would not look at her.

'Better not, Daisy,' he said at last. 'Honest, you've got to go. I shouldn't have asked you in. She was as wild as anything that time she caught us up at the railway with the Sorrel kids.'

'But why won't she let me play with you? What's the matter with me?' demanded the brown girl.

Ben looked down at the pool.

'It's because you're a nigger,' he explained shamefacedly.

The brown girl stared at him, then stamped her foot.

'I'm not a nigger,' she cried angrily. 'You've no right to call me a nigger, Benny Preedy! I'll tell my father on you. I'm not a nigger. I'm British!'

'British are white people,' mumbled Ben, and waved his hand helplessly. 'Honest, Daisy! I don't care a hoot about it. It's Mum.'

'You've no right to say it,' said the brown girl, turning her back on him and beginning to cry.

The boy was touched by her distress. He sprang to his feet and timidly touched her thin brown arm.

'Listen, Daisy,' he pleaded. 'Listen. It's not me. I don't care what colour you are. Honest I don't. I like it the way you are. It's . . . It's a nice colour!'

But the girl refused to be comforted and dragged her arm from his fingers.

'I'm just as British as you are,' she sobbed.

Looking round dismally for something to lift her out of her sorrow Ben's eyes came to rest on his harbour.

'Look here, Daisy!' he cried. 'Listen. We will make a breakwater and I'll let you do all the lighthouse—well, all the rough bits of it anyway—by yourself, if you'd like to. Do you hear me Daisy?'

The brown girl took her hands away from her eyes to consider this handsome offer, but before she could reply, one of the windows overlooking the garden was flung open, revealing, in its frame, the top half of Mrs Preedy.

A plump woman with a colourless complexion, she had just stepped out of the bath and was wearing a pale blue quilted wrapper which she held closed against her throat with one podgy white hand. On her head was a white rubber bathing cap and under this her small pale eyes glinted frostily at the children.

'Come into the house at once,' she ordered, looking straight at Ben and speaking with a small pursed mouth in a voice low but with undertones of fury. His face burning, Ben turned to obey her, and with a glare at the brown girl who was staring at her open-mouthed, Mrs Preedy slammed shut the window and dragged a curtain across it.

'How many times have I told you to keep away from that nigger family?' she demanded furiously when Ben nervously entered the room.

The corners of the boy's mouth turned down sullenly.

'But why?'

'Because I told you to,' she said sharply. 'That's quite sufficient reason!'

Sitting down by the dressing table, she put her face close to the mirror and studied her complexion; pinched her plump chin between forefinger and thumb; touched the wrinkles under her eyes.

'As if this neighbourhood wasn't bad enough without a lot of coffee-coloured rubbish scrambling about the garden,' she muttered.

Ben watched her sullenly and spoke again before he knew what he was saying.

'Daisy's a nice girl,' he burst out. 'She's pretty!'

'Pretty!' It was almost a shriek. 'That tarbrush—pretty! You don't know what you're talking about.'

'I . . .'

'Be quiet! Not another word from you! And remember, if I catch you speaking to that girl again—if I catch you so much as looking at her—you won't get out to play by yourself again until we're out of this place, which, thank goodness! can't be long now!'

Defeated, the boy sat down on the edge of the bed, while Mrs Preedy searched unavailingly for something in the drawers of the dressing-table.

'Here,' she said at last. 'Run through to the bathroom and see if I left a bottle on the top of the medicine chest. Quickly now!'

He found the bottle and brought it to her in silence.

'Now out you go,' she ordered him. 'I'm going to get dressed. Stay in the living room.'

He went out quickly, glad to escape her bitter tongue, but when she was alone Mrs Preedy did not at once put on her clothes. Instead she set about repairing the ravages wrought by soap and water on the appearance she presented to the world, and as the first step poured a measured amount of dark fluid from the bottle the boy had brought her into a white porcelain dish on the dressing-table. Then, loosening the wrapper, she bent down and with slow careful strokes began to paint her pale plump legs a warm golden brown.

TALKING POINTS

1. The first part of the story deals with the friendship between Ben and 'the brown girl' Daisy. What brings them together and what keeps them apart?
2. What aspects of Ben's character are brought out just after Daisy's breakdown?
3. What point in the developing friendship has been reached when the mother comes actively into the story?
4. The second part of the story begins with the appearance of Mrs Preedy at her window. What do you think of her remarks to her son, and what kind of person does she turn out to be? Quote words and phrases to support your opinion.
5. In the last scene in the bedroom, mother and son have a brief argument about Daisy. Discuss the two different attitudes taken up in this argument.
6. The final paragraph gives us a close-up of Mrs Preedy alone. Consider what she is doing, and say how this action is linked with the rest of the story. Comment in particular on the last seven words.
7. 'I'm not a nigger. I'm British.' 'British are white people.' These statements together make up the message or theme of the story. What is the social problem that underlies this theme?
8. Consider the different conflicts of characters in the story.
9. The writer uses dialogue or direct speech a great deal. Can you suggest why he has done this?
10. Consider again the kind of person that Mrs Preedy shows herself to be; then consider, as a contrast, the kind of girl that Daisy appears to be. Where do you think the author's sympathy lies?

Eona Macnicol

THE SMALL HERDSMAN

I found the children rough in Clachanree, even the girls. I looked with awe rather than pleasure at their spare-time activities—pushing each other down through the yawning rafters of the byre roof to fall on to the bedding bracken below, or hiding behind the half-doors and throwing screeching hens into unwary faces. My desire would go after Wattie, smaller than any of the children, yet going quietly on ways of his own.

He could often be seen here and there about An Craggoch, the croft next to my paternal grandmother's. His dry wind-bitten face was as small as a fist; below his thin neck his braces crossed so high they accentuated the tinyness of his stature: he never seemed to grow. He wore longish shorts of a ragged appearance, and went everywhere indomitably on hard bare feet.

I thought at first he was too small to play. I had the impression from his size that he was very young. Doubt came when I went up to Clachanree once in term time when all the children were at school. There in broad daylight, all young life else between walls, was Wee Wattie, tossing up bracken to dry in the sun for the cows' beds. Shocked by surprise out of observance of etiquette, I called out to him, 'What for are you not at the school, Wattie?' But I made nothing of the sheepish grin which was his only reply.

Then, seeing him close that summer on a sunny day, I noticed there was a fine soft whitish down about his cheeks, such as is on an adolescent's. His voice too, when I came to think of it, was not that of a young child. I began to wonder if he was not so much too young for horseplay, as too old.

His manner gave credence to this theory. He had the manner of a grown-up man. When he met anyone he would say, 'Well, so and so!' in the cheerful indulgent tone used by the elderly in Clachanree.

But in this gentleness there was a reserve. He seemed to stop either the playful attacks of the boys or the advances of the girls by some kind of repellent force. I never saw anyone jostle, even touch, him.

As my acquaintance with him went on, this question as to his age teased me. And once I cornered him, building up a fallen bit of the Craggoch garden wall. I did not this time ask bluntly, in the way of the world beyond, 'Wattie, how old are you?' I went more roundabout, in the way of Clachanree: 'And, Wattie, how old might yourself be, now?''

He stopped a moment from fitting the loose stones in, looked over at me, and said simply, 'How would I know?'

This gave me a delicious thrill. It was the reply a fairy changeling might have made; and it further whetted my curiosity. I reflected that Wattie, though he had quite absorbed our mode of life and outlook, and spoke in the intonations of our speech, was nevertheless not of Clachanree stock; he had come from 'the south'. His very surname was a matter of doubt, a fascinating circumstance when you came to think about it. Some said it had in any case been changed from his original one, but none could guess at the reason. After all, his Christian name was all he needed among us; among all the Donalds and Jocks and Alastairs it was distinctive enough.

He might be, if not too small, too old to play. Most certainly he was too busy. He worked constantly from morning till night. He was in the barn, in the byre, at the peat stack, in the garden, down at the well, hoeing the turnips, washing clothes at the Craggoch burn. His intelligent industry seemed to hold the Craggoch croft together. The other crofters used to talk about him: 'My, he's a proper worker, yon wee *eeshan* o' An Craggoch's!'

'An Craggoch's well served wi' yon Wee Wattie o' his!'

The labours of so small a body had an uncanniness about them. It almost seemed as if he could be in two places at once. And always he worked with such gusto and energy; he was as if possessed.

Occasionally he and An Craggoch would appear together, at times of state or ease such as the Sabbaths and Fast Days, when it was the custom in Clachanree after the three-mile walk to and from the church at Lochend to inspect, though not to work, one's fields. They presented an incongruous appearance, the tall burly crofter and his diminutive henchman side by side. It was Wattie, surprisingly, who was the spokesman of the pair. 'Well, so and so!' he would say while the other stood silent. 'We are just taking a swatch at An Craggoch's barley. It's thin the year.' Or, 'Aye, aye! Soon's the Sabbath's over, if we're spared, it's me will be having to straighten yon post in An Craggoch's fence.'

He was a silent man, An Craggoch, upright and God-fearing in a gloomy kind of way, keeping his own counsel. His sons were all away out in the great world, his wife had died. He did for himself, quite competently, though the interior of his house when I went into it reminded me of an unusually clean byre, all untidiness simply swept on one side. He must have known enough about the art of cooking for survival. Yet it seemed an austere place to rear a child, and my kind mother sometimes said it weighed on her. 'It's a cheerless place, An Craggoch's, for a young boyan. My heart is sore for yon Wee Wattie o' his.'

Her heart was very sore once when Wattie was not seen for several days. She asked An Craggoch, who was a kinsman of my father's, and was told Wattie was ill and keeping his bed. She made some dainty dish for him, a cream blancmange with lemon—she was a rare cook even on a peatfire—and a little strong chicken broth, delicately flavoured with parsley. These she carried over herself. Her offerings were politely but resolutely refused. Wattie, starting up from bed, declared he had no stomach for food, it would make him sick. I think what she really wanted was to go near him, to stroke the short straw-coloured hair, to touch the small dry face, to murmur over him the ancient half-articulate endearments she murmured in my ears when I was on the verge of sleep. But Wattie, so I gathered from my mother's hurt and puzzled look, drew back from her and plainly wished her gone.

I do not think he liked women very much; he was more distant with them than with anyone, though always courteous to a degree. The only living things he seemed to love with any warmth were An Craggoch's four cows, Daisy, Dollag, Peg and Seonaid. He kept them clean as any mother her child, and was scrupulously regular in taking them out and in. 'You could set your watch by Wattie,' my father would say as the four cows and their small herdsman would go past our windows. And for good measure, as he tended them, he would caress them with a gentle pat here, a rub there.

I had been reading, all one summer, a book of Celtic legends. I began to conceive the notion under its influence that Wattie was no child, no youth even, but an adult of some short-statured race with powers of industry beyond our own; that he was a cattleman by right of oath or conquest of An Craggoch's, his passionless devotion like that of Cuchulain for the overlord. I longed to know for sure.

So came one day when, alone and at a loose end, I saw An Craggoch's four cows come lumbering out of their byre. They climbed the rocky knoll that gave the croft its name, and stumbled clumsily down the other side with tails in the wind. Across my grandmother's greensward they went, then down the hollowed road that took the precipitous slope of the first shoulder of the hill. I remember Loch Ness far below them, at that moment deep blue in colour, with a flake of white breaking here and there over its surface. There was often an aura of expectancy about it: what might not break from that surface as the flakes of snow-white foam broke here and there?

Expectancy rose in me at any rate as I saw Wattie and his cows go down the hill. I knew the pasture he was taking them to. It was called the Lon Vorlich, a clearing among the hazel woods, not far at all from where the Eas, our waterfall river, made its way to the Loch in secret of its high over-arching trees. My mother did not like the Eas. It was forbidden me at that time ever to go there, not only because of its dangerous steep sides but because to her it had an evil atmosphere. My Gaelic was imperfect, and only in Gaelic did she ever tell ghost stories, but I think she believed there were water spirits like mermaids there. I had not often been even to the Lon Vorlich, so near the Eas's course that you could hear the sound of the water falling.

It seemed the time had come. Now, I thought, now I will go down after Wattie, and in that secluded and unearthly place I will charm the mystery of his past life from him.

I was sanguine about it because Wattie was more tolerant of me than of anyone. My very helplessness seemed to make him less liable to repel me. He would often let me watch, even accompany him in his work, always keeping a protective eye on me. 'See and keep out of the bogs, *m'eudail*,' he would bid me, 'and you in your good shoes!' Or, 'Watch yourself, Ellen. There's a loose stone in the dyke; see will the sharp edge of it fall on you.' Surely then I might prevail on him?

So I climbed over the gate, and picked my way high up on the bank above the hollowed road which was all churned and sullied by the cows, away past the covered well and across the bogs below it, and so through the low hazel and rowan trees into the Lon Vorlich. I heard the sound of the cows tearing the lush grass, the impatient whisk of their tails as they were assailed by the clegs that breed in the bracken of the surrounding slopes. And then I saw Wattie. He sat perched on a rock, unwinding a length of rope. I knew he was about to go off and cut some bracken while he was herding, so I went swiftly up to him, but quietly, scared of putting him off, and said, 'Well, Wattie!'

A smile flickered over his small face, and, 'Well, Ellen!' he said with a wealth of good-natured tolerance in his tone, coiling the rope neatly round and round his scarred forearm. He hand sickle was lying on the grass at his side. I sat down and secretly spread the skirt of my dress over it in the half-conscious hope of removing the power of his work over him.

'Wattie,' I said, 'tell me a story. Come on!'

'I donno any stories, Ellen,' he answered reasonably. 'I'm no a good scholar. I wisna that much at the school.'

'A true story, I mean.'

He shook his head, that rather sheepish smile on his lips, and was looking round for his sickle.

'Tell me about yourself then, something that happened to you.'

He paused, and gave me a wary look. 'What would be happening to me, Ellen? I was in the Home. I donno where I put——'

'Well, but before that?' I urged softly. 'What sort of place would it be you were born in?'

His eyes were on the bracken slopes and he was feeling vaguely among the grass. Still, he had not actually repulsed me. I would have to be very quiet and casual and not put him off. 'What was it like, now, where you were born? Wouldn't you be remembering anything? Anything?' I spoke as softly as I could and kept the sickle covered. His questing hand grew still.

'I mind the water——'

I had scarcely dared hope for it, but Wattie was beginning

hesitantly to speak. The constant sound of the Eas seemed to be lulling him, and he had forgotten his sickle.

'I mind the water,' he said in a tone as soft as my own.

'What water would that be?' I prompted, scarcely breathing.

'It was aye flowin',' he answered as if out of a trance. 'Flowin'. A leak it would be. Whiles it would stop, and then it would go dreep-dreep.'

There was something peculiar about his speech, but at first I did not realise what it was. My eyes fixed on him, my skirt over his sickle, I willed him to go on.

'Frae the la-avie . . . across the la-anding . . . frae wir room. And I mind the stai-airs. . . .' Fascinating! He was falling into a strange tongue. Yet I understood the gist of what he said, and listened spellbound until the image in his mind became implanted in my own, until the background dissolved round us, pasture and bracken and trees, and the hyacinthine Loch glinting between them; and we were in a dark tenement with its landing and stone stairs and a tap dripping.

The tap dripping was company for him and his brother as they crouched in their holey. . . .

'Holey?'

A cupboard under the stairs, empty except for bottles and tins. They were there so much it was like a kind of home; they seemed to pass their life there. It was very cold and damp, for it was below the la-avie, and the window opposite was broken and the rain came in. But it kept them hidden, safe—except when the wee yin coughed, he was an awfie yin for coughin'!

He was going on faster, his voice stronger, his speech stranger. He answered the question I had not asked: staggering feet coming up the stairs, loud bawling voices filling the cavity of the building. Yet here they lay still, close, till they could tell by the fumbling at the lock of their room door that danger was past.

In a pause I tried to speak, swallowing and licking my lip. But he went on, the strange accent still intensifying so that it was as much by intuition as by understanding that I grasped his meaning. When they got too hungry the wee yin would cry. Wattie must venture out, his heart in his mouth, and watch until the door opened, then slip in and seize whatever he could to make a meal. He was terrified he would be shut in and the wee yin be left alone.

'Wattie,' the effort to speak was like the effort in a nightmare. He turned to me, but his eyes were sightless, and went on speaking, his voice rising now in pitch until it was like the voice of a young child. Once or twice neighbours must have taken them in. He minded one time because of an oddity: it was pouring and the rain was driving into the holey; the man from the flat below had said, 'Jeese! Them weans is drooken wet,' and taken them into his room. There was a fire, a brown teapot on the hob and sausages jumping in a fryingpan, a smell to take the mice from the walls. The woman set them down on stools and gave them plates of sausages which they gulped down, and then a kind of fruit out of a tin with a sweet 'clarty' juice, and cream on it. But at the third mouthful of this he began to feel sick, the wee yin was already boakin'.

'Wattie,' I broke through my nightmare, 'didn't you have anyone to look after you?'

A wee dog sometimes came and lay beside them in the holey. It smelt something awfie and it started them itching, but it was a rare wee dog.

'But who looked after you? Hadn't you a mother?'

Again he turned blindly towards me, and answered in the shrill voice, 'Deed aye had we! Who my faither wis I never kenned, but we had wir mither. She was a ba-ad yin!' I put my hands over my eyes, but it was my ears I should have covered, for it was the words in the high strange speech that conjured up the evil visions: drunken brawling and obscene caresses and violence. 'It wis after a hammering he got the wee yin sickened. They took him away in the ambulance. They said he wis deid.' I must have got a cry out, and tried to struggle to my feet, for he said with something of his old gentleness, 'Na, I wisna sorry. He wis aye greetin' and coughin'. He wis a chairge on me. I didna mind.'

Then suddenly the angle of his head altered, the thin neck was stretched out, his eyes started, his mouth twisted in a grimace that showed his teeth. He said in a loud screaming cry, 'It wis the dog I minded!' He moved his head from side to side, crying words I had never heard before nor ever have heard again. 'The dirty drunken brutes, they hanged my dog on me! They tied one end o' the belt round his neck and threw it o'er the pulleys. And when I went for them they had me on the floor, and they all got their hands on me pulling me this way and that, laughin' and roarin', and herself the worst o' the lot. And then——

'And then——' He had put his two hands round his thin neck. I was compelled to understand what he was saying. I was in his power now, not he in mine. I could not stop him, could not escape from going down with him into his remembered hell. Successful in hanging the dog, they started on Wattie himself. But neighbours must have intervened; for he woke, gasping in agony, having gone all the way to the end of life and back again.

When I came to myself I was gasping too, my sobs strangling my breath. I was in terror I would never get back into my own life again. Yet the fearful incantation was over, Wattie was gone from my side. And slowly round me was forming the familiar scene: the damp pasture, the high arches of the Eas trees, and down below through the hazels, far down, the creeping water of the Loch greyed with evening.

Still I could not move, not even to rub away the burning tears that ran over my face.

It was Wattie himself who released me. I found him

standing beside me, his sickle in his hand. His head poked forward from the enormous load of bracken on his back, so that he was comically like a tortoise in shape. Cheerful and dignified as ever, he looked at me and gently reproved me, 'What for are you sitting there all the time crying, Ellen? Rise now like a good lassie. It is time to be taking up An Craggoch's cows.'

GLOSSARY

croft:	small farm	*weans:*	children
eeshan:	nipper	*swatch:*	close look
m'eudail:	(literally, cattle) my darling, my treasure (Gaelic)	*drooken:*	soaked, drenched
		clarty:	sticky, messy
dreep dreep:	drip drip	*boakin':*	belching (noise made by someone about to be sick)
la-vie:	lavatory, toilet		
wee yin:	small one	*greetin':*	weeping
awfie:	awful		

TALKING POINTS

1. The story emerges from the relationship between the young girl who narrates and Wattie, the Small Herdsman. What are we told in the first paragraph that might explain why the girl is drawn to Wattie?
2. What different aspects of Wattie's character are revealed during the first part of the story dealing with his life—and his illness—at An Craggoch?
3. What led Ellen to pursue Wattie to find out about this past? What ideas had she formed herself on the subject?
4. How does Ellen show her skill and sensitivity in persuading Wattie to reveal his past life?

5. At this point we enter an entirely different world which is marked by a change of language, Wattie's 'strange tongue'. What is there in Wattie's story that makes the reader (a) inquisitive, (b) amused, (c) horror-stricken, (d) sympathetic, and (e) disgusted?
6. What are our feelings about Wattie after his account of his past life? What becomes clear about Wattie's attitude (a) to his mother, (b) to the 'wee yin' and (c) to his dog?
7. What incident would you say marks the climax in Wattie's story? What effect does this have on Ellen? In what sense then is the climax to Wattie's story also the climax to the whole story?
8. At the end of the story we return to the highland setting. What points of contrast between country and town life have been brought out by the story?
9. Read the last paragraph again, and consider particularly Wattie's last words. In what sense is Wattie 'releasing' Ellen? What makes the last sentence spoken by Wattie a 'good' ending to the story?
10. Consider the whole story again. What effect do you think the experience of re-living Wattie's past may have on himself and on Ellen?

J. F. Hendry

THE DISINHERITED

A ray of sun, from behind a cloud, opened out on a small figure in a suit of blue Harris tweed, hastening desperately along the empty streets, between the shadowing tenements, to reach the haven of church before the bell stopped ringing. A pale ghost,with bloodless lips sailed past the dark-blue windows of Templeton's the Grocers, Benson's the Newsagents, and the Hill Café, now and then, as it ran, staring backward, appalled, at a reflection in their window-blinds. A cap bit deep into the brow, and a spotted bow-tie pointed to five past seven. There was no time to adjust them.

——Dong! Ding-dong! Ding-dong!——sang the chimes, their echoes washing in waves of monotonous warning up the High Street, where a yellow cat stood lazily stropping itself against a chalk-fringed wall.

—— Dong! Ding-dong!—— and then, surprisingly, in a sudden giddy recoil, stopped altogether. Sawney broke into a run as he tackled the cobbled hill.

'What's the hurry?' called Big Sneddon, the policeman, from across the street. 'Ye're awfu' religious all of a sudden, or are ye off to a fire? The Bad Fire?——'

He broke down into raucous laughter at his own wit, but the face which was turned on him was so full of savagery, and something else besides, that it would have silenced anyone, let alone Big Sneddon, the handcuff-king. The angular blue figure straightened at once, and gazed thoughtfully after Sawney, now racing uphill, but it was not the expression alone in the latter's face that had sobered him. 'Poor Devil,' he said aloud, 'he's for it all right.'

Panting as he arrived at the door, Sawney paused for a moment or two, feeling as breathless as the bells. He turned to the east, but only for the wind, and, taking off his bonnet, waved it once or twice before his face, to dry the sweat.

'Late! Curse it,' he coughed, then plunged, like a man in a dream, through the open portals of the Kirk.

In their pew, the family were sitting waiting for him. He walked down the aisle, conscious of their hostile stares, and saw his mother's face grow slowly purple. He was wearing high, narrow boots of red ox-hide, which creaked as he walked, and now seemed about to crack, though this was hardly a cause for anger. His father, however, to his surprise, blew his nose loudly in his handkerchief, and Jimmy, his brother, sniggered outright, in the aisle. It was just like Jimmy to snigger. He had neither tact nor sympathy. He needed a doing!

Grinning sheepishly to several of his mother's stairhead acquaintances, he took his place beside her on the cushion, and a long and vicious hair entered his leg. He squirmed.

'How dare ye,' hissed his mother. 'Sawney, how dare ye drag me down like this! Never, never, will I be able to live doon the disgrace ye've brought upon me this day!'

Why this should be so was not immediately clear to Sawney, since, just then, in a river of robes, the Minister entered through a side-door and flowed up the stairs that led to the pulpit. You would have thought he was going to his execution, the majestic way he walked up.

These ruminations were cut short by a fierce dig in the ribs. 'Ye're finished, dae ye hear? I want no part of ye from now on! Oh, wait till I get ye outside,' his mother moaned in whispering, inarticulate rage, one eye on the pulpit where the Minister was opening the Book— 'I'll skivver the liver out o' ye, ye impiddent young deevil! Look at ye, look at your face!'

His father's impassive stare, Jimmy's noble contempt, his mother's passion and the amused glances of young girls, peeping over the tops of their hymn-books, at last forced Sawney actually to feel his face, which had in fact, now that his attention had been drawn to it, begun to seem slightly puffy.

Only then, as the congregation, without warning, stood up like a forest to sing the opening hymn: 'Be Strong in the Fight!' did it dawn on Sawney's horror-stricken conscience that he had come to church, to attend morning service, with two black eyes.

They swelled up till he could scarcely see. Miserably he sat as though in a cage, exposed to amusement, curiosity and scorn, his hands thrust between his knees, out of sight, to still their convulsive bird-like movements of escape.

Whenever he turned to look at her, he met the fixed glare of his mother, or heard the words: 'Vagabond! Scamp!——'

He grued when he thought of the end of the service, when he would have to face her tigerish wrath, out there in the bright sunlight. Surely this enforced silence would do something to calm her down? Instead, it only served to deepen her shame.

'The disgrace!' she said, drawing her breath, and looking round, her back stiff.

Sheepishly, he grinned again and looked at his father, who pushed forward his white moustache and stolidly gazed at the pulpit.

Once more, he was in disgrace. He had always been in disgrace ever since, a boy in striped pants, called 'Zebra' by his unfeeling friends, he had left school for the last time and kicked his books high in the air over the wall into Sighthill Cemetery. The only prize he had ever had in his life, was a book called *No and Where to Say It,* and that was for regular attendance at the Highland Society School. It was a good book. It told you about the perils of life for a young man, and how easy it was, after the first weak 'Yes' to evil companions, to go on saying 'Yes', and end up gambling, drinking, going with women and spending your substance, or breaking your mother's heart.

'You'll break my heart!' she hissed now. 'You and your wild hooligan freens!——'

He had learned to say 'No' from that book. Surely *he* could not be breaking his mother's heart? He did not drink. He did not gamble. All he did was box every Sunday morning in the stables behind Possil Quarry.

He was not, Sawney told himself, in the habit of grousing, but what chance had he ever had? Instead of meditating now on his sins, as he should have done, or trying to remember exactly what it was that Joseph had taken with him from Pharaoh's palace, he began to think of his own upbringing. An old man, who had once been an agricultural labourer, wearing a lum hat wanting a crown, had stood like a clown in the cobbled backyard of the house in Grafton Street when he was born, his patron saint, an industrial troubadour, singing in beggared chivalry. In token of the day of infinite jest it was, he played on a flute that through his mother's dreams had drowned the sound of the traffic, and now and then quavered a thoroughly commercial chorus:

Balloons and windmills for jelly jars!

Amid that great conglomeration of city streets, blocks of tenements, unsightly factories, and engineering shops, intricate as the network of railways imposed on the town without so much as a by-your-leave, without planning of any sort, and with no principles at all save those of immediate and substantial gain, there was no one to suckle the child except the midwife, a stout buxom woman, timeless as one of the Furies, as it lay blinking in the bed on the wall.

Outside his room lay the rampant scenery of loch and mountains but Campsie and Lennoxtown were as far away, for the child, as the life his ancestors had once led among these former fields. Their miles had been transformed into money. Nearer were the forests of poverty broken down into the fuel and ash of hoardings, blossoming enormous letters and pictures, a mythology of commerce, whose gods and demons waited to invade his fairyland. Nearer were the woodland paths of tramlines and railways. An iron song of bells and sirens stilled the birds. He had been born into a cage.

Nomadic crime had settled on these steppes. Where once the total police force had consisted of Sergeant Oliver and Constable Walker, now twenty-six officers and men were required to keep what they called 'the peace', a force larger than that of other equally populated areas further south—such as Ayr.

His self-pity was cut rudely short.

A thunder of shuffling presaged the 'skailing' of the kirk. The congregation relaxed and allowed itself the luxury of starched smiles.

Sawney rose, and filtered slowly and shamefully, out into the bright sunlight, feeling more forsaken, more forlorn than ever.

Outside, little groups stood discussing the sermon, waiting for friends, inspecting each other's dress, or gossiping. Mrs Anderson sailed past them, her ears burning, imagining that behind her she could hear suppressed laughter, scandalous allegations and even criminal threats.

She waited until she had reached the comparative neutrality of the pavement, then she spun round on her son, who had been dragging behind like an unwilling puppy.

'How did it happen? Who did it to ye? It serves ye right!' she said in one breath.

'It wasna my fault, honest! He hit me first.'

'Who? I'll never, *never* forgive ye for this, I swear!'

'Dukes Kinnaird. He was sparring. He's to fight the English champion tomorrow. They asked me to go a couple of rounds with him.'

'Did ye?' asked the white-haired old man who was his father, stuffing thick black down into his pipe and trying to look angry, in support of his wife.

'It was only supposed to be a spar,' pleaded Sawney, 'but all of a sudden he hit me right between the eyes. I saw he was coming for a knock-out, the dirty dog.'

'Don't dare use that language in front of me. On a Sunday, too!'

'What happened?' his father asked.

'I let go with my left and crossed with my right. He went back over the ropes into a bath of hot water.'

The old man laughed. His wife turned on him. 'That's enough of you! Well, I'm for no more of it. Ye can come hame and pack yer things. I don't want ye in my hoose. Ye'll end up on the end of a rope one day, I tell ye.'

For all his waywardness, Sawney was genuinely appalled. Leave home? Where would he go? He'd be a laughing stock. He knew his mother, the auld wife, was hard, but only now was he beginning to realize just how hard. She seemed to have no affection for him left.

'Ye'll pack your things and away this very night!' she said.

He looked at the auld wife to see if she meant it. Her collar stood high on her scrawny neck, and her hat, with one feather on it, made her seem a comical figure, in her anger.

'Why can't you be liker your brother?' his father asked in a low voice. 'He never gets into any scrapes.'

'We canny all be in the Post Office,' said Sawney.

'He's a well-behaved lad. It's a pity ye werena liker him. He'll do weel for himself.'

Sawney did not doubt it. He had never denied that his brother was a very worthy man, a gentleman, and different altogether from himself. It had seemed natural to him, even as a boy, that he should have to fight Jimmy's battles, although Jimmy was older than he was, in the days when fights really were fights. Many a 'jelly-nose' he had awarded boys at school to save his brother's reputation and the family honour, but it never occurred to him to talk about it, or to think there was any particular merit in it. Jimmy was the meritorious one. He never got into scrapes, never fought, never squabbled. Such things were beneath him. He read books until they wafted him into the Post Office, and now he was a Sorter—to Sawney, one of the intellectuals.

As they walked down Hillkirk Road, Mrs Anderson bowing in enforced silence, and screwing up her eyes in what she imagined to be a smile to her neighbours, he had to step on to the pavement to avoid a horse and cart, which with a great grinding of the brake was proceeding downhill. It reminded him of early escapades, which really, he thought, had been enough to break even his mother's stout heart. Had he been younger, he would almost certainly have jumped on the back of that same lorry. He had always done so, until the fatal day when he slipped and the wheel went over his leg, breaking it. He had then had to spend six weeks in bed. What a delight it had been to get out again!

He could still remember that afternoon as clearly as this one. It had been such heaven to run about with his leg out of plaster of Paris, that he must have gone slightly mad. Another lorry passed, and forgetting his mother's injunctions, he had darted after it as soon as he was out of the close-mouth. Leaning on the back with his stomach, he heaved himself up, putting one foot on the rear-axle as he did so. To his horror, his foot slipped and slid through between the spokes. He had howled, for the bone was broken, for the second time. Then, far more scared of his mother than of what had happened to his foot, he had limped upstairs into the close, and sat for three-quarters of an hour on the stairhead lavatory seat, white and sick, gazing at the blood on his leg and hoping somehow it would heal before he had to go in. It did not heal, and he had had a thrashing on top of the ordeal.

Now they were in Springburn Road and Mrs Anderson could give something like full vent to her fury.

'I've a good mind to belt your ear!' she said. 'If you were half a man you'd dae it!' she concluded to her husband.

'But he's a man!' protested the latter. 'He's past that!' Then seeing the ruthlessness in his wife's features, he came to a firm resolve.

'All right,' he said, 'I'll take him in hand myself.'

'You will,' she repeated, 'and he'll go this very night, don't forget!'

'How could you do it? To me? Your own mother? Don't I work and slave for ye? Haven't I always worked and slaved to bring you up in decency?'

She was working herself up into a frenzy, starting a 'flyting', and Sawney sought for a way of escape, any way of escape.

'You told me to come to Church, so I came!' he parried.

'You came! You came did ye? Do ye know what the neighbours will be saying this verry meenit? Do ye?'

'Excuse me, mither,' he said, 'there's Rob across the street. I want to talk to him. See you later!'

As he dashed across the roadway to Rob, he heard his mother's last few words hurtle after him.

'Ye can come and fetch yer things when ye're ready!'

It was late when Sawney finally arrived home, having put off the evil hour as long as he possibly could. The door was locked. But it was not the first time he had been locked out, and he knew what to do. Prising open the bedroom window, he climbed up and firmly grasped the aspidistra plant he knew stood there, so that it should not fall over. Then, stepping in, he advanced with it in his arms, through the darkness, into the middle of the room. There was a loud crash.

He had walked bang into the half-open door. Now the fat was in the fire! For a second there was silence, then:

'Come here!' thundered his father's voice from the kitchen.

Walking awkwardly through, the plant still in his hand, he saw the old man standing firmly by the gas-bracket, in his shirt-sleeves, with his cap on.

'I've come to get my things,' he said sullenly. '———are they upstairs?'

'A fine time to come in I must say! Yer things? I've done all *your* packing, my lad! There's nothing left for you to do. It's all here for you to take!'

He had never seen his father so determined before. It was an unpleasant shock. He had no idea where he would go in the middle of the night, unless to Rob's. He saw his father peer forward, as though to read his mood, and an unreasoning anger took hold of him:

'I'm not going to give up boxing because of her,' he said defiantly. 'Where are my things?'

'Ye can do whatever ye like. It's up to you,' was the answer. 'Your things? How many things dae ye think ye've got, beyond what ye stand up in, ye pauper? There's your things, the lot of them!'

He nodded towards the mantelpiece. Sawney's eyes followed.

'There's only a matchbox there!' he said.

His father's features relaxed. 'I ken that,' he answered, knocking out his pipe, 'but it's big enough to hold a' *you* own!'

They stared at each other, and ruefully smiled.

His father put his fingers on the gas-bracket.

'Try not to upset your mother again!' he said. 'Are you a' right?'

'All right,' said Sawney, about to speak, but his father had already turned down the gas and the little kitchen was in complete darkness.

By the red glare of the fire they made their way to bed.

GLOSSARY

The Bad Fire:	hell
doing:	a telling-off or a beating-up
skivver:	cut, stab, pierce
grued:	shuddered, shivered so that the skin crept
lum hat:	top hat
skailing:	emptying
ken:	know
scrawney:	scraggy, thin
canny:	cannot
jelly-nose:	bloody nose
close-mouth:	doorway of tenement opening on to street
flyting:	scolding, wrangling
meenit:	minute

TALKING POINTS

1. What exactly does the opening sentence tell us? Consider particularly the effect of such words as 'small', 'desperately', 'empty', 'haven'.
2. Talk about the brief part Big Sneddon plays in the story. What kind of a person does he appear to be?
3. What is the mystery about Sawney's appearance that the author cleverly hints at before it is revealed? Who reveals it? Comment on the humorous link between this revelation and the title of the hymn.
4. Sawney, feeling a bit sorry for himself, has a kind of day-dream about his misfortunes and past life. What do you think the author is suggesting about Sawney by introducing (a) the old man who sang and played the flute when Sawney was born, (b) the city setting, (c) the country setting, and (d) the increased crime of the area?
5. Outline the two different points of view, the mother's and Sawney's, about boxing. What is there to be said in favour of each?

6. Sawney's brother is in marked contrast to Sawney. What are the main points of this contrast? Where do you think the author's sympathies lie?
7. Consider the part played by the father in the story. What is his attitude (a) to his wife, and (b) to Sawney? Are there any signs of sympathy between father and son?
8. The final scene takes the form of a conversation in the kitchen between father and son. Comment on the way the father deals with the situation, and consider the significance of the match-box.
9. The main events of the story occur in three different settings—streets, church, home. Consider how well each setting suits the events of each part.
10. Comment on the last sentence as an ending to the story: 'By the red glare of the fire they made their way to bed'.

Edward Scouller

MURDOCH'S BULL

Indeed you wouldn't be far wrong if you said that Murdoch loved that bull. On a winter's night he would come into its stall and speak to it like it was a Christian, quietening it when the glare of his lamp in its red eyes made the brute stamp and rattle its chain. In the Gaelic he would talk to it, you know, calling it the silliest names that nobody uses except to a baby or maybe to a girl. And he would catch one of those great spreading horns of its and pull the shaggy hair that hung down over its eyes and rub his big, three-fingered hand up and down its forehead. The beast would snort and stare at him till it saw that this was just Murdoch that wouldn't do it any harm. Then he would stoop his head and the two of them, the savage bull and the half-witted lad, would rub their brows together.

Of course, there was no harm in Murdoch, no harm whatever. It was just the queer bit that was in all the Portmor MacLachlans. There was his old grandmother now, Giorsal Pharuig, her that reared Murdoch after his mother went off to the mainland—and Dear knows where she is now, but the father was killed before ever Murdoch was born. Giorsal was queer too: she would never leave that dirty old black house of hers down Portmor, and the new laird building the grand house for her in Glasard with a slated roof and water pipes in the sink and all. She was no companion for a growing boy, but who else was there to do anything for him? Everybody has their own troubles to look after.

The bull belonged to old Giorsal. And what she wanted

with a brute like that and her with only six cows and a farm no bigger than a croft was what everybody in the island often wondered. Maybe it was just because Murdoch made such a work with it. He was just twelve when the bull was born, and he helped Miall Dubh and Calum with the calving: he was a knowledgeable lad with cattle even if they'd never managed to get a word of schooling into him. By the time the bull was four years old there wasn't his like in Mara, no nor in all the Hebrides. He stood fifteen hands high and must have weighed anything up to fourteen hundred pounds. Yellow he was, and with those huge horns of his and the broad chest and the short legs he was a perfect picture. But what use was he to Giorsal? He was just going to waste on a small place like Portmor, or indeed on the island of Mara at all. And then he got so wild too. You daren't come within half a mile of the MacLachlan's place without making sure of where he was. There was no use of keeping near a dyke either, for he'd leap dyke or gate like a dog rounding up sheep.

Well, when old Giorsal died—rest her soul!—Murdoch came to the Grants at Killoran. And the bull came with him. Of course, it was good of the Grants to take the orphan boy in, but he was worth his keep anywhere. He couldn't be trusted with a message, but he could do a man's work and more in the fields, and at night when he wasn't on the hills with that bull he'd sit in the barn playing on his mouth-organ. A lovely player he was too, and quick to pick up a tune.

In the long run folk began to complain about Murdoch's bull. It wasn't so bad for us that knew about it and that knew the likeliest roads to keep clear of it when we were near Killoran. But poor old Rory Mor that had to cross the Grants' land to get from the shore to his house was in terror of his life of the brute. Twice it chased him on his way home from the lobsters. It would have been laughable if it hadn't been a shame to see the old man so frightened. There was once it went after him and he just got into his hen-house and no more. The bull couldn't get through the door for its horns, but it stood roaring and foaming and throwing up the turfs with its feet and the sparks nearly flying out of its eyeballs. Seumas Grant and two of the men tried to drive it back with hayforks, but it turned on them and scattered them too. In the end it was poor silly Murdoch they had to send for. He was only fifteen at the time. They kept shouting at him to be careful, but he just walked right up to the bull and caught it by the horns and turned it round and walked away with it.

But that wasn't the funny bit of the story. Murdoch wouldn't ever talk to Rory after that, because, he said, Rory must have been annoying the poor bull. The Grants tried to bring him round to let it be sold, for they were people that never liked to bother or be bothered by anybody. But Murdoch, that was namely through the island for his gentleness and good temper, he flew into such a rage that they thought he'd take a fit. He swore he'd kill anybody that laid a finger on his bull to sell it.

Of course it got more and more vicious as it grew older. But the more people talked against the beast the more Murdoch doted on it. Poor lad, he was so proud of being the only one on the island that could manage this bull. It made him twice as fond of it to know that it made folk respect him that more often laughed at him. You would even see him walking along beside it with his arm across its neck and him gabbling away to it more than he ever talked to the folks at the farm. Of course nobody talked much to poor Murdoch at any time. He was a quiet, decent, biddable lad; but he had such a ganching tongue that it wasn't easy to know what he was saying, and it wasn't often worth knowing anyhow.

At last there was a terrible to-do about the bull. It chased some of the summer visitors from the hotel and tossed one of them into the loch. The laird happened to be in Mara at the time, and the visitors and the hotel folk complained to him.

So on the Sunday he set out himself to see the Grants and Murdoch. The Grants were away into Scalasaig to church, and Murdoch was out in the fields as usual with his bull when the laird arrived.

He came on the pair of them there, and you would have thought the animal knew what he was come about. The bull was as quiet and gentle as an old collie. He even let the stranger stroke his nose. And Murdoch in his ganching, mixed-up way telling the laird all the time there was no harm in the bull, only folk wouldn't let it alone. So in the long run the laird said he could keep it for a while if he'd watch it better when strangers were about.

Poor Murdoch was so glad to get keeping his bull that he couldn't get a word out of him for the ganch-ganching and stuttering. So the laird bid him good-bye and turned to walk back to the road. He hadn't gone twenty steps when the bull down with its head, up with its tail and went after him with a noise like thunder. Before Murdoch could even shout to it to stop, it had its head under the laird and flung him into the middle of a whin bush. It was a mercy he wasn't killed. But Murdoch got hold of the bull and quietened it while the laird struggled up and got on to the road.

There was only one thing for it after that: the bull had to be either killed or sold. They got a buyer for it quick enough, a man over in Oban that was buying for an Australian. The night the bull went away, half the island of Mara was along to see what pranks it would play on the road. Everyone swore it would kill someone before they got it out on the ferry-boat to the *Dunara.* It was the middle of the night when they brought it from Killoran, but at every door you could see women and children peering out; the men were all helping with the bull. They had put a ring in its nose with a rope to it, and they had tied one hind foot to a fore one. Every man had a thick stick, and two or three had forks. There were four or five dogs. It was a queer sight to see the whole of them jogging along in the dark, their lanterns bobbing up and down, and all of them keeping one eye on the bull and one on the side of the road.

And there was the famous bull in the middle of them walking along as tame and quiet as a kitten. Maybe it was dazed with all the lights and the crowd, or maybe it was wondering where it was going. Or maybe it knew it was finished with its tantrums in Mara. You can never tell what a bull's thinking, or whether it's thinking at all. It walked on the ferry as if it had been doing nothing else all its life, and didn't even struggle much when they put the belly-straps on it and slung it on to the steamer.

They could hardly get Murdoch off the *Dunara.* He cried, and he cried, just like the big senseless baby he was, and wanted to take the bull back ashore with him. However, they got him away at last, and he went off the ferry and up the road roaring and weeping. Of course folk said he'd soon forget about the bull, because he was just like a baby in everything but his size and strength, and babies soon forget.

But Murdoch didn't seem to forget. He wouldn't speak to anybody. He just went prowling about the barn and the byre and the hills at all hours of the day and night, and wouldn't play on his mouth-organ, not even to please Mrs Grant that had always been able to understand him and work with him.

Then one night he didn't come to the kitchen for his porridge at supper-time, and in the morning they got his body all battered and broken in the water below the cliffs at Kilchattan. Maybe he fell over: he was only a silly lad after all.

GLOSSARY

black house: a primitive highland dwelling

ganching: stammering, stuttering, speaking inarticulately

TALKING POINTS

1. The first three paragraphs form a kind of introduction to the story: we hear about Murdoch's relationship with the bull, go back to the time of the grandmother Giorsal, and then have a description of the bull itself. Pick out interesting details from each section; then work out your own first impressions of Murdoch. In what ways is he unusual as hero or central figure?
2. What words in the opening sentence does the author use to get on familiar terms with the reader?
3. 'It was just the queer bit that was in all the Portmor MacLachlans.' What part does that queer bit play in the story?
4. What exactly happened to old Rory Mor? What, according to the narrator, *was* 'the funny bit' of that story?
5. Why did the bull mean so much to Murdoch?
6. Often in a short story the sequence of events leads up to an important happening which forms the crisis or turning-point. What is the crisis, or shattering experience, in Murdoch's story?
7. Consider the scene describing how the bull was taken away on the *Dunara*. What do you find comic about this scene, and what tragic?
8. 'But Murdoch didn't seem to forget.'
   Read the last two paragraphs again, and then consider what was happening to Murdoch after the bull had been taken away. Does the death of Murdoch seem a 'right' ending to the story?
9. Talk about the last sentence—its suggestion as to what might have happened, its final comment on Murdoch. Is its tone cold or cruel?

10. Discuss (a) the kind of people we meet in the story as supporting characters, (b) their background and way of living, and (c) the events that specially appeal to you. Quote words or phrases that suggest it is a highlander using English who is telling a story of his own community.

Fred Urquhart

ALICKY'S WATCH

Alexander's watch stopped on the morning of his mother's funeral. The watch had belonged to his grandfather and had been given to Alexander on his seventh birthday two years before. It had a large tarnished metal case and he could scarcely see the face through the smoky celluloid front, but Alexander treasured it. He carried it everywhere, and whenever anybody mentioned the time Alexander would take out the watch, look at it, shake his head with the senile seriousness of some old man he had seen, and say: 'Ay, man, but is that the time already?'

And now the watch had stopped. The lesser tragedy assumed proportions which had not been implicit in the greater one. His mother's death seemed far away now because it had been followed by such a period of hustle and bustle: for the past three days the tiny house had been crowded with people coming and going. There had been visits from the undertakers, visits to the drapers for mourning-bands and black neckties. There had been an unwonted silence with muttered 'sshs' whenever he or James spoke too loudly. And there had been continual genteel bickerings between his two grandmothers, each of them determined to uphold the dignity of death in the house, but each of them equally determined to have her own way in the arrangements for the funeral.

The funeral was a mere incident after all that had gone before. The stopping of the watch was the real tragedy. At two o'clock when the cars arrived, Alexander still had not got over it. He kept his hand in his pocket, fingering it all through the short service conducted in the parlour while slitherings and muffled knocks signified that the coffin was being carried out to the hearse. And he was still clutching it with a small, sweaty hand when he took his seat in the first car between his father and his Uncle Jimmy.

His mother was to be buried at her birthplace, a small mining village sixteen miles out from Edinburgh. His father and his maternal grandmother, Granny Peebles, had had a lot of argument about this. His father had wanted his mother to be cremated, but Granny Peebles had said: 'But we have the ground, Sandy! We have the ground all ready waiting at Bethniebrig. It would be a pity not to use it. There's plenty of room on top of her father for poor Alice. And there'll still be enough room left for me—God help me!—when I'm ready to follow them.'

'But the expense, Mrs Peebles, the expense,' his father had said. 'It'll cost a lot to take a funeral all that distance, for mind you we'll have to have a lot o' carriages, there's such a crowd o' us.'

'It winna be ony mair expensive than payin' for cremation,' Granny Peebles had retorted. 'I dinna hold wi' this cremation, onywye, it's ungodly. And besides the ground's there waiting.'

The argument had gone back and forth, but in the end Mrs Peebles had won. Though it was still rankling in his father's mind when he took his seat in the front mourning-car. 'It's a long way, Jimmy,' he said to his brother. 'It's a long way to take the poor lass. She'd ha'e been better, I'm thinkin', to have gone up to Warriston Crematorium.'

'Ay, but Mrs Peebles had her mind made up aboot that,' Uncle Jimmy said. 'She's a tartar, Mrs Peebles, when it comes to layin' doon the law.'

Although Alexander was so preoccupied with his stopped watch he wondered, as he had so often wondered in the past, why his father and his Uncle Jimmy called her Mrs Peebles when they called Granny Matheson 'Mother'. But he did not dare ask.

'We have the ground at Bethniebrig, Sandy,' mimicked Uncle Jimmy. 'And if we have the ground we must use it. There'll still be room left for me when my time comes.' The auld limmer, I notice there was no word aboot there bein' room for you when *your* time comes, m'man!'

Alexander's father did not answer. He sat musing in his new-found dignity of widowerhood; his back was already bowed with the responsibility of being father and mother to two small boys. He was only thirty-one.

All the way to Bethniebrig Cemetery Alexander kept his hand in his pocket, clasping the watch. During the burial service, where he was conscious of being watched and afterwards when both he and James were wept over and kissed by many strange women, he did not dare touch his treasure. But on the return journey he took the watch from his pocket and sat with it on his knee. His father was safely in the first car with Mr Ogilvie, the minister, and his mother's uncles, Andrew and Pat. Alexander knew that neither his Uncle Jimmy nor his Uncle Jimmy's chum, Ernie, would mind if he sat with the watch in his hand.

'Is it terrible bad broken, Alicky?' asked James, who was sitting between Ernie and his mother's cousin, Arthur.

'Ay,' Alexander said.

'Never mind, laddie, ye can aye get a new watch, but ye cannie get a new——'

Ernie's observation ended with a yelp of pain. Uncle Jimmy grinned and said: 'Sorry, I didnie notice your leg was in my way!'

The cars were going quicker now than they had gone on the way to the cemetery. Alicky did not look out of the windows; he tinkered with his watch, winding and rewinding it, holding it up to his ear to see if there was any effect.

'Will it never go again, Alicky?' James said.

'Here, you leave Alicky alone and watch the rabbits,' Ernie said, pulling James on his knee. 'My God, look at them! All thae white tails bobbin' aboot! Wish I had a rifle here, I'd soon take a pot-shot at them.'

'Wish we had a pack o' cards,' said Auntie Liz's young man, Matthew. 'We could have a fine wee game o' Solo.'

'I've got my pack in my pocket,' Ernie said, raking for them. 'What aboot it, lads?'

'Well——' Uncle Jimmy looked at Cousin Arthur; then he shook his head. 'No, I dinnie think this is either the time or the place.'

'Whatever you say, pal!' Ernie gave all his attention to James, shooting imaginary rabbits, crooking his finger and making popping sounds with his tongue against the roof of his mouth.

The tram-lines appeared, then the huge villas at Newington. The funeral cars had to slow down when Clerk Street and the busier thoroughfare started. James pressed his nose against the window to gaze at the New Victoria which had enormous posters billing a 'mammoth Western spectacle'.

'Jings, but I'd like to go to that,' he said. 'Wouldn't you, Alicky?'

But Alicky did not look out at the rearing horses and the Red Indians in full chase. He put his watch to his ear and shook it violently for the fiftieth time.

'I doubt it's no good, lad,' Uncle Jimmy said. 'It's a gey auld watch, ye ken. It's seen its day and generation.'

The blinds were up when they got back, and the table was laid for high tea. Granny Matheson and Granny Peebles were buzzing around, carrying plates of cakes and tea-pots. Auntie Liz took the men's coats and hats and piled them on the bed in the back bedroom. Alicky noticed that the front room where the coffin had been was still shut. There was a constrained air about everybody as they stood about in the parlour. They rubbed their hands and spoke about the weather. It was only when Granny Matheson cried: 'Sit in now and get your tea,' that they began to return to normal.

'Will you sit here, Mr Ogilvie, beside me?' she said. 'Uncle Andrew, you'll sit there beside Liz, and Uncle Pat over there.'

'Sandy, you'll sit here beside me,' Granny Peebles called from the other end of the table. 'And Uncle George'll sit next to Cousin Peggy, and Arthur, you can sit——'

'Arthur's to sit beside Ernie,' Granny Matheson cut in. 'Now, I think that's us all settled, so will you pour the tea at your end, m'dear?'

'I think we'd better wait for Mr Ogilvie,' Granny Peebles said stiffly. And she inclined her head towards the minister, smoothing the black silk of her bosom genteelly.

Alicky and James had been relegated to a small table, which they were glad was nearer to their Granny Matheson's end of the large table. They bowed their heads with everyone else when Mr Ogilvie started to pray, but after the first few solemn seconds Alicky allowed himself to peek from under his eyelashes at the dainties on the sideboard. He was sidling his hand into his pocket to feel his watch when Tiddler, the cat, sprang on to the sideboard and nosed a large plate of boiled ham. Alicky squirmed in horror, wondering whether it would be politic to draw attention to the cat and risk being called 'a wicked ungodly wee boy for not payin' attention to what the minister's sayin' about yer puir mammy,' or whether it would be better to ignore it. But Mr Ogilvie saved the situation. He stopped in the middle of a sentence and said calmly in his non-praying voice: 'Mrs Peebles, I see that the cat's up at the boiled ham. Hadn't we better do something about it?'

After tea the minister left, whisky and some bottles of beer were produced for the men, and port wine for the ladies. The company thawed even more. Large, jovial Uncle Pat, whose red face was streaming with sweat, unbuttoned his waistcoat, saying: 'I canna help it, Georgina, if I dinna loosen my westkit I'll burst the buttons. Ye shouldna gi'e fowk sae much to eat!'

'I'm glad you tucked in and enjoyed yourself,' Granny Peebles said, nodding her head regally.

'Mr Ogilvie's a nice man,' Granny Matheson said, taking a cigarette from Uncle Jimmy. 'But he kind o' cramps yer style, doesn't he? I mean it's no' like havin' one o' yer own in the room. Ye've aye got to be on yer p's and q's wi' him, mindin' he's a minister.'

'Ye havenie tellt us who was all at the cemetery,' she said, blowing a vast cloud of smoke in the air and wafting if off with a plump arm. 'Was there a lot o' Bethniebrig folk there?'

'Ay, there was a good puckle,' Uncle Pat said. 'I saw auld Alec Whitten and young Tam Forbes and——'

'Oh, ay, they fair turned out in force,' Uncle Jimmy said.

'And why shouldn't they?' Granny Peebles said. 'After all, our family's had connections with Bethniebrig for generations. I'm glad they didnie forget to pay their respects to puir Alice.' And she dabbed her eyes with a small handkerchief, which had never been shaken out of the fold.

'I must say it's a damned cauld draughty cemetery yon,' Uncle Andrew said. 'I was right glad when Mr Oglivie stopped haverin' and we got down to business. I was thinkin' I'd likely catch my death o' cauld if he yapped on much longer.'

'Uncle Pat near got his death o' cauld, too,' Uncle Jimmy grinned. 'Didn't ye, auld yin?'

'Ay, ay, lad, I near did that!' Uncle Pat guffawed. 'I laid my tile hat ahint a gravestone at the beginnin' of the service and when it was ower I didna know where it was. Faith, we had a job findin' it.'

'Ay, we had a right search!' Uncle Jimmy said.

'It's a pity headstones havenie knobs on them for hats,' Auntie Liz said.

'Really, Lizzie Matheson!' cried Granny Peebles.

Auntie Liz and the younger women began to clear the table, but Alexander noticed that Auntie Liz did not go so often to the scullery as the others. She stood with dirty plates in her hands, listening to the men who had gathered around the fire. Uncle Pat had his feet up on the fender, his large thighs spread wide apart. 'It's a while since we were all gathered together like this,' he remarked, finishing his whisky and placing the glass with an ostentatious clatter on the mantelpiece. 'I think the last time was puir Willie's funeral two years syne.'

'Ay, it's a funny thing but it's aye funerals we seem to meet at,' Uncle Andrew said.

'Well, well, there's nothin' sae bad that hasna got some guid in it,' Uncle Pat said. 'Yes, Sandy lad, I'll take another wee nippie, thank ye!' And he watched his nephew with a benign expression as another dram was poured for him. 'Well, here's your guid health again, Georgina! I'm needin' this, I can tell ye, for it was a cauld journey doon this mornin' frae Aberdeen, and it was a damned sight caulder standin' in that cemetery.'

Alexander squeezed his way behind the sofa into the corner beside the whatnot. Looking to see that he was unnoticed, he drew the watch cautiously from his pocket and tinkered with it. As the room filled with tobacco smoke the talk and laughter got louder.

'Who was yon wi' the long brown moth-eaten coat?' Uncle Jimmy said. 'He came up and shook hands wi' me after the service. I didnie ken him from Adam, but I said howdyedo. God, if he doesnie drink he should take doon his sign!'

'Och, thon cauld wind would make anybody's nose red,' Matthew said.

'Ay, and who was yon hard case in the green bowler?' Ernie said.

'Ach, there was dozens there in bowlers,' Uncle Jimmy said.

'Ay, but this was a *green* bowler!'

Uncle Jimmy guffawed. 'That reminds me o' the bar about the old lady and the minister. Have ye heard it?'

Alexander prised open the case of the watch, then he took a pin from a small box on the whatnot and inserted it delicately into the works. There was loud laughter, and Ernie shouted above the others: 'Ay, but have ye heard the one about——?'

'What are ye doin', Alicky?' James whispered, leaning over the back of the sofa.

'Shuttup,' Alexander said in a low voice, bending over the watch and poking gently at the tiny wheels.

'I dinnie see why women can't go to funerals, too,' Auntie Liz said. 'You men ha'e all the fun.'

'Lizzie Matheson!' Granny Peebles cried. 'What a like thing to say! I thought ye were going to help your mother wash the dishes?'

It was going! Alicky could hardly believe his eyes. The small wheels were turning—turning slowly, but they were turning. He held the watch to his ear, and a slow smile of pleasure came over his face.

'What are you doing there behind the sofa?'

Alexander and James jumped guiltily. 'I've got my watch to go!' Alicky cried to his father. 'Listen!'

'Alexander Matheson, have you nothing better to do than tinker wi' an auld watch?' Granny Peebles said. 'I'm surprised at ye,' she said as she swept out.

Abashed, Alicky huddled down behind the sofa. James climbed over and sat beside him. They listened to the men telling stories and laughing, but when the room darkened and the voices got even louder the two little boys yawned.

They whispered together. 'Go on, you ask him,' James pleaded. 'You're the auldest!'

James went on whispering. Beer bottles were emptied, the laughter and the family reminiscences got wilder. And presently, plucking up courage, Alexander went to his father and said: 'Can James and I go to the pictures?'

There was a short silence.

'Alexander Matheson,' his father cried. 'Alexander Matheson, you should be ashamed o' yersel' sayin' that and your puir mother no' cauld in her grave.'

'Och, let the kids go, Sandy, Uncle Jimmy said. 'It's no' much fun for them here.'

'We're no' here for fun,' Alexander's father said, but his voice trailed away indecisively.

'You go and put the case to your granny, lad, and see what she says,' Uncle Jimmy said. He watched the two boys go to the door, then looking round to see that Mrs Peebles was still out of the room, he said: 'Your Granny Matheson.'

Five minutes later, after a small lecture, Granny Matheson gave them the entrance money to the cinema. 'Now remember two things,' she said, showing them out. 'Don't run, and be sure to keep your bonnets on.'

'Okay,' Alicky said.

They walked sedately to the end of the street. Alicky could feel the watch ticking feebly in his pocket, and his fingers caressed the metal case. When they got to the corner they looked round, then they whipped off their bonnets, stuffed them in their pockets, and ran as quickly as they could to the cinema.

GLOSSARY

onywye:	any way
limmer:	objectionable woman, harridan
cannie:	cannot
gey auld:	rather old
puckle:	number
havenie:	haven't
havering:	talking nonsense
tile hat:	top hat
ahint:	behind
syne:	ago
guid:	good
nippie:	small whisky
bar:	story, anecdote

TALKING POINTS

1. In the first part of the story we view the two 'tragedies' from the point of view of nine-year-old Alicky. In what sense was the stopping of the watch 'the real tragedy'? Is Alicky a heartless boy, or can his concern for his watch be justified?
2. The funeral scenes make up the second part of the story. What do we learn here about certain members of the family?
3. Trace the stages of the behaviour of the grown-ups during and just after the funeral tea, and say why you think the author drops Alicky almost out of sight at this point.
4. What aspects of family gatherings does the author stress in the scene that follows the funeral tea?
5. Consider how the author gradually brings Alicky and James back into the picture, and how he builds up the climax of the watch re-starting.
6. What changes had come over the family group when Alicky plucked up courage to ask permission to go to the cinema?

7. Discuss the contrast in character between the two grannies, especially in the last scene before the boys leave for the cinema. Which granny would you prefer to deal with, and why?
8. What kind of mood was Alicky in by the end of the story? What led to this mood? Consider in what sense the story may be regarded as rounded off by the last paragraph.
9. Think again of the two big themes of the story—the two 'tragedies'. Can you think of any deeper meaning that the author may intend in the stopping of the watch when it did and in its re-starting when it did? Is there a central message to the story?
10. Instance points in the story where the reader might be expected to feel (a) amusement, (b) sadness, (c) sympathy, (d) mild shock, (e) annoyance, (f) pessimism, and (g) tolerance.

Iain Crichton Smith

THE TELEGRAM

The two women—one fat and one thin—sat at the window of the thin woman's house drinking tea and looking down the road which ran through the village. They were like two birds, one a fat domestic bird perhaps, the other more aquiline, more gaunt, or, to be precise, more like a buzzard.

It was wartime and though the village appeared quiet, much had gone on in it. Reverberations from a war fought far away had reached it: many of its young men had been killed, or rather drowned, since nearly all of them had joined the navy, and their ships had sunk in seas which they had never seen except on maps which hung on the walls of the local school which they all had at one time or another unwillingly attended. One had been drowned on a destroyer after a leave during which he had told his family that he would never come back again. (Or at least that was the rumour in the village which was still, as it had always been, a superstitious place.) Another had been drowned during the pursuit of the *Bismarck*.

What the war had to do with them the people of the village did not know. It came on them as a strange plague, taking their sons away and then killing them, meaninglessly, randomly. They watched the road often for the telegrams.

The telegrams were brought to the houses by the local elder who, clad in black, would walk along the road and then stop at the house to which the telegram was directed. People began to think of the telegram as a strange missile pointed at them from abroad. They did not know what to associate it with, certainly not with God, but it was a weapon of some kind, it picked a door and entered it, and left desolation just like any other weapon.

The two women who watched the street were different, not only physically but socially. For the thin woman's son was a sub-lieutenant in the Navy while the fat woman's son was only an ordinary seaman. The fat woman's son had to salute the thin woman's son. One got more pay than the other, and wore better uniform. One had been at university and had therefore become an officer, the other had left school at the age of fourteen.

When they looked out the window they could see cows wandering lazily about, but little other movement. The fat woman's cow used to eat the thin woman's washing and she was looking out for it but she couldn't see it. The thin woman was not popular in the village. She was an incomer from another village and had only been in this one for thirty years or so. The fat woman had lived in the village all her days; she was a native. Also the thin woman was ambitious: she had sent her son to university though she only had a widow's pension of ten shillings a week.

As they watched they could see at the far end of the street the tall man in black clothes carrying in his hand a piece of yellow paper. This was a bare village with little colour and therefore the yellow was both strange and unnatural.

The fat woman said: 'It's Macleod again.'

'I wonder where he's going today.'

They were both frightened for he could be coming to their house. And so they watched him and as they watched him they spoke feverishly as if by speaking continually and watching his every move they would be able to keep from themselves whatever plague he was bringing. The thin woman said:

'Don't worry, Sarah, it won't be for you. Donald only left home last week.'

'You don't know,' said the fat woman, 'you don't know.' And then she added without thinking, 'It's different for the officers.'

'Why is it different for the officers?' said the thin woman in an even voice without taking her eyes from the black figure.

'Well, I just thought they're better off,' said the fat woman in a confused tone, 'they get better food and they get better conditions.'

'They're still on the ship,' said the thin woman who was thinking that the fat woman was very stupid. But then most of them were: they were large, fat and lazy. Most of them could have better afforded to send their sons and daughters to university but they didn't want to be thought of as snobbish.

'They are that,' said the fat woman. 'But your son is educated,' she added irrelevantly. Of course her son didn't salute the thin woman's son if they were both home on leave at the same time. It had happened once they had been. But naturally there was the uneasiness.

'I made sacrifices to have my son educated,' said the thin woman. 'I lived on a pension of ten shillings a week. I was in nobody's debt. More tea?'

'No thank you,' said the fat woman. 'He's passed Bessie's house. That means it can't be Roddy. He's safe.'

For a terrible moment she realised that she had hoped that the elder would have turned in at Bessie's house. Not that she had anything against Bessie or Roddy. But still one thought of one's own family first.

The thin woman continued remorselessly as if she were pecking away at something she had pecked at for many years. 'The teacher told me to send Iain to University. He came to see me. I had no thought of sending him before he came. "Send your son to university," he said to me. "He's got a good head on him." And I'll tell you, Sarah, I had to save every penny. Ten shillings isn't much. When did you see me with good clothes in the church?'

'That's true,' said the fat woman absently. 'We have to make sacrifices.' It was difficult to know what she was thinking of—the whale meat or the saccharines? Or the lack of clothes? Her mind was vague and diffused except when she was thinking about herself.

The thin woman continued: 'Many's the night I used to sit here in this room and knit clothes for him when he was young. I even knitted trousers for him. And for all I know he may marry an English girl and where will I be? He might go and work in England. He was staying in a house there at Christmas. He met a girl at a dance and he found out later that her father was a mayor. I'm sure she smokes and drinks. And he might not give me anything after all I've done for him.'

'Donald spends all his money,' said the fat woman. 'He never sends me anything. When he comes home on leave he's never in the house. But I don't mind. He was always like that. Meeting strange people and buying them drinks. It's his nature and he can't go against his nature. He's passed the Smiths. That means Tommy's all right.'

There were only another three houses before he would reach her own, and then the last one was the one where she was sitting.

'I think I'll take a cup of tea,' she said. And then, 'I'm sorry about the cow.' But no matter how you tried you never could like the thin woman. She was always putting on airs. Mayor indeed. Sending her son to university. Why did she want to be better than anyone else? Saving and scrimping all the time. And everybody said that her son wasn't as clever as all that. He had failed some of his exams too. Her own Donald was just as clever and could have gone to university but he was too fond of fishing and being out with the boys.

As she drank her tea her heart was beating and she was

frightened and she didn't know what to talk about and yet she wanted to talk. She liked talking, after all what else was there to do? But the thin woman didn't gossip much. You couldn't feel at ease with her, you had the idea all the time that she was thinking about something else.

The thin woman came and sat down beside her.

'Did you hear,' said the fat woman, 'that Malcolm Mackay was up on a drunken charge? He smashed his car, so they say. It was in the black-out.'

'I didn't hear that,' said the thin woman.

'It was coming home last night with the meat. He had it in the van and he smashed it at the burn. But they say he's all right. I don't know how they kept him out of the war. They said it was his heart but there was nothing wrong with his heart. Everyone knows it was influence. What's wrong with his heart if he can drink and smash a car?'

The thin woman drank her tea very delicately. She used to be away on service a long time before she was married and she had a dainty way of doing things. She sipped her tea, her little finger elegantly curled in an irritating way.

'Why do you keep your finger like that?' said the fat woman suddenly.

'Like what?'

The fat woman demonstrated.

'Oh, it was the way I saw the guests drinking tea in the hotels when I was on service. They always drank like that.'

'He's passed the Stewarts,' said the fat woman. Two houses to go. They looked at each other wildly. It must be one of them. Surely. They could see the elder quite clearly now, walking very stiff, very upright, wearing his black hat. He walked in a stately dignified manner, eyes straight ahead of him.

'He's proud of what he's doing,' said the fat woman suddenly. 'You'd think he was proud of it. Knowing before anyone else. And he himself was never in the war.'

'Yes,' said the thin woman, 'it gives him a position.' They watched him. They both knew him well. He was a stiff, quiet man who kept himself to himself, more than ever now. He didn't mix with people and he always carried the Bible into the pulpit for the minister.

'They say his wife had one of her fits again,' said the fat woman viciously. He had passed the Murrays. The next house was her own. She sat perfectly still. Oh, pray God it wasn't hers. And yet it must be hers. Surely it must be hers. She had dreamt of this happening, her son drowning in the Atlantic ocean, her own child whom she had reared, whom she had seen going to play football in his green jersey and white shorts, whom she had seen running home from school. She could see him drowning but she couldn't make out the name of the ship. She had never seen a really big ship and what she imagined was more like the mailboat than a cruiser. Her son couldn't drown out there for no reason that she could understand. God couldn't do that to people. It was impossible. God was kinder than that. God helped you in your sore trouble. She began to mutter a prayer over and over. She said it quickly like the Catholics, O God save my son O God save my son O God save my son. She was ashamed of prattling in that way as if she was counting beads but she couldn't stop herself, and on top of that she would soon cry. She knew it and she didn't want to cry in front of that woman, that foreigner. It would be weakness. She felt the arm of the thin woman around her shoulders, the thin arm, and it was like first love, it was like the time Murdo had taken her hand in his when they were coming home from the dance, such an innocent gesture, such a spontaneous gesture. So unexpected, so strange, so much a gift. She was crying and she couldn't look . . .

'He has passed your house,' said the thin woman in a distant firm voice, and she looked up. He was walking along and he had indeed passed her house. She wanted to stand up and dance all round the kitchen, all fifteen stone of her, and shout and cry and sing a song but then she stopped. She couldn't do that. How could she do that when it must be the thin woman's son? There was no other house. The thin woman was looking out at the elder, her lips pressed closely together, white and bloodless. Where had she learnt that self-control? She wasn't crying or shaking. She was looking out at something she had always dreaded but she wasn't going to cry or surrender or give herself away to anyone.

And at that moment the fat woman saw. She saw the years of discipline, she remembered how thin and unfed and pale the thin woman had always looked, how sometimes she had had to borrow money, even a shilling to buy food. She saw what it must have been like to be a widow bringing up a son in a village not her own. She saw it so clearly that she was astounded. It was as if she had an extra vision, as if the air itself brought the past with all its details nearer. The number of times the thin woman had been ill and people had said that she was weak and useless. She looked down at the thin woman's arm. It was so shrivelled, and dry.

And the elder walked on. A few yards now till he reached the plank. But the thin woman hadn't cried. She was steady and still, her lips still compressed, sitting upright in her chair. And, miracle of miracles, the elder passed the plank and walked straight on.

They looked at each other. What did it all mean? Where was the elder going, clutching his telegram in his hand, walking like a man in a daze? There were no other houses so where was he going? They drank their tea in silence, turning away from each other. The fat woman said, 'I must be going.' They parted for the moment without speaking. The thin woman still sat at the window looking out. Once or twice the fat woman made as if to turn back as if she had something to say, some message to pass on, but she didn't. She walked away.

It wasn't till later that night that they discovered what had happened. The elder had a telegram directed to himself, to tell him of the drowning of his own son. He should never have seen it just like that, but there had been a mistake at the post office, owing to the fact that there were two boys in the village with the same name. His walk through the village was a somnambulistic wandering. He didn't want to go home and tell his wife what had happened. He was walking along not knowing where he was going when later he was stopped half way to the next village. Perhaps he was going in search of his son. Altogether he had walked six miles. The telegram was crushed in his fingers and so sweaty that they could hardly make out the writing.

TALKING POINTS

1. The opening 'shot' (in terms of cinema) shows us two figures sitting at a window overlooking the village street. What aspects and contrasts of character does the author suggest by likening one woman to 'a fat domestic bird' and the other to a buzzard or 'more aquiline' type of bird?
2. The second and third paragraphs fill in the background of the story by describing the effect of the war on the village. Pick out and talk about some of the important details given here.
3. What was the significance of a telegram in the lives of the people of the village? (Remember the author tells us that they thought of a telegram as 'a strange missile' or 'a weapon of some kind'.)
4. Discuss the differences in attitude and point of view that keep the women apart. What, on the other hand, brings them together?

5. The progress of the local elder bearing the telegram is interrupted by the talk of the women at the window. Describe the stages in this 'progress', and pick out what you think are the important topics of conversation.
6. What do you take to be the crisis of the story? In what sense is this an anti-climax? Consider also in what sense the elder's tragedy makes the story more moving.
7. Look at the last sentence again. How is the state of the telegram related to the experiences of the two women?
8. In a short story, characters can undergo an experience that alters their lives. What are the vital features of the central experience in this story, and how might the women have been changed by this experience?
9. What characteristics or references or clues are there that would enable you to place the story in a particular part of Scotland? What kind of community is suggested?
10. Try to work out the main events of the story in terms of cinema, referring to opening shot, cross-cutting for contrast, close-ups, long shots, zooming shots, tracking shots. On what would you fade out?

John Thomas Low

JEMIMA

There were five of us on this expedition to the hills—Dave and his wife Helen, my wife Sandra, and myself—and Jemima. She of course was different from the four of us: she was a creature of metal and rubber with leather upholstery for clothes—but still a creature. Most people would have called her a motor-bicycle and side-car; but we knew better: we called her Jemima—for Dave had assured us she had a soul.

'She's a grand cratur,' he told us the evening before our climb on Cairn Toul, 'mony's the ploy I've been on wi' auld Jemima. I've toured most of Scotland on her back; and she's never let me doon yet. The strange thing is—she seems to be at her best on hill tracks. I certainly wouldna dream of gaun aff to the hills withoot her. . . '

'But that's surely jist plain ridiculous,' I interrupted, rather brusquely, 'that auld rickle o' rubber and tin micht easily brak doon—miles from nowhere—and then where wad ye be?'

The women were inclined to agree but Dave was not in the slightest put out: he looked at the three of us steadily, and with a mild air of complete self-confidence said, 'I suppose it's gey difficult for you folks to understand, but the great thing to grasp is this: Jemima doesna brak doon. Mony's the time I've come down off the hill fair exhausted. . .'

Dave's story was again interrupted—this time by the arrival of Mrs McLeod with the dinner. Soon a mellowness had descended upon us as we turned from the table to the fireside to beguile the lazy hours until bedtime. In haphazard fashion we made plans for the climb.

'We'll save a good hour by drivin' up the glen on Jemima,' pronounced Dave with pride.

'Oh, no, Dave, please,' said his wife.

'Why not, Helen? Ye ken what Jemima is capable of doing—'

'But is the road good enough for a motor-bike?' asked Sandra, my wife, 'I've heard that the scree is a bit loose—a mile or so up the glen.'

'Aye,' said I, 'and there's been a lot o' rain recently. There micht be a landslide, and we dinna want Jemima to be stranded—'

'Jemima—stranded!!' Dave's scorn fair silenced us all. 'Listen to me, a'body. Jemima's a motor-bike wi' a soul; and she has the soul of a climber.'

That seemed to settle the matter: Jemima was enrolled as the fifth member of the company.

And indeed next morning as the September sun shone brilliantly, we felt glad after all that Jemima would be taking us quickly into the heart of the hills for an early start on the climb. What a heavily-laden cratur she was as she chugged and girned her way up from the Ey cottage, lassies and rucksacks in the side-car and myself perched insecurely on the pillion. We came to a sudden and unaccountable stop not two miles from our base; yet such was Dave's loving skill that he had the old lady on her wheels again in a few short minutes. Badly jolted and shaken though we were we could enjoy the sight of the lower hills in the distance and the sparkling Dee on the left.

Just when we had become accustomed to this bouncing, up-and-down kind of locomotion, Dave suddenly stopped and shut off the engine.

'This is as far as we'll tak' her,' he declared firmly.

'But, man, it's a few miles yet to the White Bridge—' I began.

'I ken, but the track gets worse hereabouts. Jemima has a

stout hert: she could do it; but there are four of us, and we maun think o' the cratur's health. We'll just leave her here.'

There was nothing more to be said. After disembarking we watched with detached interest the antics of Dave as he manoeuvred Jemima a little distance off the road to find a suitable open-air garage. The old lady spluttered a sigh or two, then settled down to her vigil. Glinting in the sun there she seemed to be keeping a watch-dog's eye on us as we prepared for our walk to Cairn Toul.

Boots felt heavy but hearts were light as we swung along the upper part of the Old Glen, past the White Bridge, and on to the hill path proper.

When we cried in past Corrour Bothy we found the place deserted; and it was with relief that we turned away towards the ridge that leads to the summit of Cairn Toul. As I approached that summit with the company spread out behind me, I felt it exciting to look back along the ridge with its steep drop on either side and to admire the back-cloth view of Ben Macdhui and, hundreds of feet below, the tiny thread of the Dee flowing down the Lairig Ghru.

We stood on the top of Cairn Toul at four-thirty on a late September day and enjoyed mighty vistas to west and south. We were in the very heart of the mountain sanctuary of Scotland.

I think it was my crazy idea that we should descend by the back way and come out at the head of Glen Geusachan. It was quite a pleasant route but must have added an hour or so to our time; for, when we reached the water, darkness was already falling and the stars were beginning to twinkle. When at length we were once more on the right side of the Dee (which was really the left side gaun doon!) it seemed a miracle to blunder on to the path, for by now it was quite dark, and we were stumbling drunkenly over boulders and heather.

Yet what a grand nicht it was to be abroad in! The blue-black of the sky was inlaid with a million tiny diamonds; and at our feet the worms were carrying their torches, for the moon was otherwise engaged. From the river, only half-visible in a kind of black gleam, came the sounds not only of its gentle rush, but also of the eerie bellowing of the deer.

Then—slowly, insidiously—the stars covered themselves up, the glow-worms went out, and the air became heavy and oppressive. The first distant flash of lightning and the answering growl of thunder sent a thrill along our spines. Then it broke in all its fury: sheets and forks of violent light rent the sky; the growls became rumbles and the rumbles pounding crashing cannons of noise that caused even the well-set Cairngorms to quake. And it rained: quietly at first, then steadily, then heavily—then splashingly. The Deil—his ain mountain stood just behind us—was having wild fun with the switchboard, the thunder sheets, and the rain machine of his own open-air theatre.

We trekked, trudged and trembled through all this, thoroughly soaked, thoroughly frightened. At times we huddled together to shelter from the wet and to shut out the blinding flashes; then we would stagger on, occasionally shouting remarks that were quickly swept away and drowned in rain and thunder. Finally, utterly exhausted, we came to rest on a big boulder near the top of an incline. Here we would bide; we felt we could go no farther. Then it happened. A tremendous double flash suddenly lit up the whole scene. We saw the river, the enclosing hills, the path, and—at the top of the rise—a shapeless mass with bars of metal that flashed back miniature lightning of its own. Dave and I quickly rose and made our way up to it. Could it be? Another flash revealed it unmistakably. Yes, it was her—it was she—the one and only—Jemima. No doubt the wee folk had been at their tricks: how they had dragged her up to the head of the glen to this high point was too much for us storm-befuddled mortals to work out. But—there she was. She had come to meet us—the gallant soul!

Dave had already mounted his beast; and soon the noise of spluttering Jemima and the flashing of her headlights were vying with the storm.

'Good old Jemima! I telt ye, didn't I? Jemima to the rescue!'

And he went on shouting until his wife told him to haud his gab. Jemima was somehow manoeuvred down on to the Glen track; and we all prepared to climb on board. The rain had lessened; the White Bridge nearby revealed itself starkly in occasional flashes of lightning; but although the thunder continued to growl like a sulky dog, we knew the climax had passed. Once we had all taken our places Jemima roared into action, and off we set down towards home and food.

Dave was enjoying himself at the controls: he opened out and let Jemima go tearing down that ancient highway at tremendous speed. We were reminded of Tam o' Shanter's Ride. We skelped on through dub and mire haudin' fast to our bonnets, certainly not fearing warlocks or wee folk but blessing them rather for the help they had given us. Dave was croonin' some auld Scots sonnet, but I was thinking of the legend of the Erl King:

> Who rides so late through night and wind,

when suddenly there was a violent sensation of crunching and crashing, and Jemima stopped dead.

'What's wrang noo, Dave, for goodness' sake?' asked his wife.

'Jist come oot and see.'

Boulders of all shapes and sizes loomed up in front of us, and an occasional flash from the dying storm showed that the road was well and truly blocked. I tried to rouse the others from their dismay.

'Well come on. We'll a' lend a hand and try to move Jemima over the stones.'

Tired though we were, we went to the task with a will. We pushed and tugged at Jemima; we groaned and grunted and strained, but all to no avail. After half an hour of this kind of work, we were fit to drop, and decided to give it up. We lifted out our packs, bade Jemima a reluctant farewell, and took the road once more.

In the morning we looked out at the firs and the moorland and the Dee sparkling in the sunlight, and thought of Jemima up there waiting to be rescued. Off we set then after breakfast, and found the track in bad condition: there had been many falls of scree and the ground was very wet—running streams everywhere. Then we reached a great heap of boulders, and just as we were struggling laboriously across the stony wilderness, we caught sight of the glint of metal. Quickly we made our way towards her; but what a sad sight met our eyes! Jemima seemed firmly, immovably, eternally embedded in the scree. Her handlebars, seat and part of the side-car were visible; but she appeared to be in process of settling down in her Cairngorm sepulchre. Poor Jemima! Dave and I removed our battered hats. We were all now completely converted: Jemima had a soul; her heart was in the Cairngorms, and she had found an appropriate resting-place.

I was quite unprepared for the change that took place in Dave's attitude a few weeks later. When I met him at King's College one Saturday morning he began to discuss Jemima in the most callous way.

'They managed to clear the track, Wull; and Jemima was brocht hame.'

'Well, go on,' I sniffed.

'Bob Milne bocht Jemima. Guess hoo much I got for her?'

'What, ye've sold Jemima?' It sounded the most dreadful sacrilege; and I was so miserable that I didna hear the exact sum that he announced with such pride. He rattled on.

'And what d'ye think, Wull?' I've bocht a wee car—jist the thing for the glens at the back o' beyond. The cratur has a stout hert—I'm thinkin' she'll tak' to the hills as Jemima did.'

'Just a minute, Dave. Fa did ye say bocht Jemima?'

'Bob Milne. Ye ken him surely? He's a great climber—'

'Yes, I know. And was he tellin' ye he climbed Cairn Toul recently on his way to Rothiemurchus? *He* was caught in a thunderstorm jist as we were.'

'Eh, that's queer.' Dave paused. His enthusiasm had gone; he was for once subdued and thoughtful. Then a light seemed to dawn in his eyes.

'Ye ken, Bob said something that I didna' richtly understand at first. Now I'm beginnin' to see daylicht.'

'And what was't he said, Dave?'

'He said something aboot being in love with Jemima ever since he had found her on the Glen Road and she had helped him up the hill—on the day of the thunderstorm.'

GLOSSARY

cratur:	creature
ploy:	activity, employment
gaun aff, doon:	going off, down
rickle:	loose collection
brak doon:	break down
gey:	rather, very
dinna:	don't
girned:	complained, grumbled
maun:	must
cried in past:	called at
ain:	own
bide:	stay
telt:	told
haud his gab:	hold his tongue
skelped:	rushed, drove, dashed
haudin':	holding
warlocks:	wizards
brocht:	brought
bocht:	bought
fa:	who

TALKING POINTS

1. The prologue to the story takes place on the evening before the mountain walk. What is Dave's plan to save time on the walk, and why do the others disagree with him? Consider his attitude to Jemima.
2. The real action of the story begins next morning. How was the first part of the journey accomplished, and why was it so abruptly concluded? Quote words or phrases to show that Jemima is now being humorously regarded by the narrator himself as a living creature.
3. Even up to the point where darkness overtakes the party there is a sense of enjoyment of the mountain walk. What would you consider the highlights of the experience so far?
4. In the next part of the mountain walk the sense of enjoyment is completely destroyed. This is where the drama begins to mount. Pick out words or phrases that the author uses to convey the violence of the storm. Why do you think he refers to the Devil (the 'Deil') here?
5. A high climax comes when the party are exhausted and have almost given up the struggle. Why is the sight of Jemima so dramatic and unexpected? Who are the wee folk, and what might they have done? What other fanciful explanation is hinted at?
6. In the next part describing the return journey on Jemima, the story develops a great pace and a feeling of excitement that remind the author of Tam o' Shanter's ride and the legend of the Erl King. Can your suggest another reason why these old tales should be mentioned at this point?
7. The end of the mountain story is presented as a short rescue scene next morning. Discuss the state of the track, and the effect on the party of seeing Jemima in her

'Cairngorm sepulchre'. What do you think the author means by this phrase?

8. The last part of the story could be regarded as an epilogue or a tailpiece with a twist. It describes the meeting of Dave and the narrator 'a few weeks later'. Discuss the reversal of roles—Dave's changed attitude to Jemima, and Wull's 'grief'. In what respect is Dave still the old Dave?
9. Talk about the part played by Bob Milne in the story. What is suggested as a rational explanation for the apparently supernatural happening?
10. Part of the humour of the story depends on accepting Jemima as a living creature. Read the story again; then describe Jemima's imagined qualities and trace the course of her adventures.

George Mackay Brown

THE FERRYMAN

At noon on Martinmas day, disinherited, I left Mirdale—my brother's wife sending her spiteful mirth after me across three fields, and the old man cold with spite in his grave—and turned my steps in the direction of the Hall. The factor could offer me one job only, to row the boat *Lupin* between the island and the town with any passengers who might wish to cross.

At that time of year, the threshold of winter, Hoy Sound is often stormy, crammed with wave and squall, and a tide runs broken and abrupt from the Atlantic into Scapa Flow and back again, twice a day.

I agreed to take charge of the boat until such time as Joe the ferryman recovered from his broken leg.

The next morning I waited a while at the rock, smoking, before anybody came. A man walked along the beach with his face muffled and ordered me to take him across. I looked into the suffering eyes of Josie of Taing.

'I have the toothache in my jaw,' he said, 'and no man in this island can pull the rotten tooth out. My teeth are too deep in my skull. But they say the blacksmith in Stromness has fingers like nut-crackers.'

I rowed Josie across for sixpence.

At the pier of Stromness were three girls with a basket of herring who wanted to sell their fish in the island.

They were helping each other aboard the *Lupin,* chattering like starlings, when a dark hooded man walked down the slip and said: 'Behold, is this the ferry to the wicked Godforsaken island across the firth?'

When the three girls saw the black Bible under his arm they scrambled back on to the pier; for it is and always has been a thing of small luck to travel on the sea with a preaching man.

The preacher did not open his mouth all the way across. He sat in the stern and read his Bible. I didn't care for the look of the man. He didn't offer to pay his fare, and to tell the truth I was afraid to ask him. Still thumbing his Bible he stepped ashore and went swaying up the beach over the slippery stones. 'May your preaching prosper,' I shouted after him. 'It's a wicked island you've come to, and be sure to visit the croft of Mirdale. The worst woman in Orkney lives there.'

I sat on the thwart till noon smoking my pipe and nodding, and then didn't the two hawkers who have been scrounging and threatening and stealing their way through Hoy and Flotta and Graemsay since the middle of October come up to me as silent as otters. 'Take us to Stromness,' said the man.

'Sixpence each,' I said.

'We're poor wandering people,' said the woman. 'I have the black cough in my throat this week past.'

'A shilling for the two,' I said, 'if that sounds any better.'

'You have an unlucky look about you,' said the man. 'It isn't likely you'll see age.'

'Half a florin,' I said, 'and that's as low as I'll come.'

All the way across they sat in the bow muttering to each other, and every now and then sending a black look across at me.

At last they stood on the steps at Stromness pier, and the hawker woman turned to skirl at me as sharp as a gull, 'May your boards fall asunder in the middle of Hoy Sound, and may the mouth of the shark be under you that day!'

The three herring girls ran down the pier out of the pub, red in the face with porter. They scrambled on board the *Lupin* with shrieks and grey flurries of skirt. Their names were

Margaret, Annie and Seenie. They laughed most of the way across the Sound. Seenie took a half-bottle of rum from her skirt pocket and we all began to drink, the flask going from mouth to mouth. Margaret was sick in the middle of the Sound. The other three of us finished the rum. Seenie threw the empty half-bottle into the tide-race. I did not charge a fare. They gave me a bunch of herring for nothing.

I sat on the beach of the island smoking, my arms so stiff with rowing I could hardly lift my pipe to my teeth. It had been a fine blue day, but now the wind turned into the east and blew grey gurls over the Sound.

At ten past three there was a plaintive outcry mixed with cursing and swearing from the road above, and then appeared Mansie of Cott dragging a grey ewe over the tangle.

'I'm taking her,' he said, 'to the butcher in Stromness, and God help me, I'm loath to part with her. She's been a good ewe and dropped a dozen fine lambs, but Jessie-Bella wants a new coat and hat for the kirk on Sabbath. Truth to tell, I would rather the ewe was safe in her field and it was Jessie-Bella I was taking to the butcher in Stromness.'

I took sixpence for Mansie's fare and threepence for the sheep.

I had hardly pushed the sharny backside of the beast off the boat when who set his boot on the rocking thwart but the Stromness police sergeant, Long Rob.

'Turn your boat round quickly, my man,' said Long Rob. 'The law's required this day in the island.' He had a blue paper, a summons, sticking out of his pocket.

By now the wind was racketing round the corners of the houses and tearing the gulls out of their clean circles.

'Is it the black preacher you're after?' I said.

'It is not,' said Long Rob.

'It wouldn't be the woman of Mirdale you're going to arrest?' I cried in sudden wild hope.

'It's Tom of Braewick,' said he, 'that must face the sheriff on Tuesday first for having no licence for his motor-bike.'

'That'll be sixpence for your fare,' I said, and I wish I had never spoken, for I had to sign my name on a form in two places—a difficult thing for me at any time—stating that I had duly received the above-mentioned sum; and the boat jumping and stotting all over the Sound with the rising rage of the sea.

By the time I set the sergeant ashore in the island the sky was as purple as squashed grapes. I began to pull the *Lupin* up over the wet stones.

Only a fool, I thought to myself, will want to travel on a night like this! The thought had hardly shaped itself in my mind when six men came out of the gloom with a coffin on their shoulders. 'This is Williamina of Bewsley,' said Frank the undertaker. 'She's to be buried in Stromness, where she came from, tomorrow morning. If you ask me she's been in this island fifty years too long.' With that he put a sixpence on the lid of the coffin.

So I ferried Williamina of Bewsley across the waters of death. It was a black passage. Six other men were waiting at Stromness for the coffin. They lifted it without a word on to their shoulders and walked solemnly up the pier, the street lights falling dreich on to them till they turned up the close to the house where the dead woman had been born seventy years before.

Spray was flying across the harbour like smoke. I tied up the *Lupin* at the pier and slept that night on a truss of straw in the cattle shed.

I dreamt of the cornfields of Mirdale.

GLOSSARY

clarty:	dirty	*dreich:*	dismally, drearily
stotting:	bouncing		

TALKING POINTS

1. The first sentence is remarkable for the amount of information it gives the reader. What do we learn from it—particularly about the situation of the ferryman-narrator?
2. Talk about the setting of the story, and consider how it affects the kind of job the narrator has been given.
3. When an author adopts the 'I' method of story-telling he reveals his own assumed character. Discuss the qualities of the ferryman that are revealed by his encounters with his various passengers.
4. What comment about island and domestic life may the author be making in relating the episode of Mansie of Cott?
5. 'So I ferried Williamina of Bewsley across the waters of death.'
   Consider how the author builds up to this climax of his story, and say how far you think this last journey provides a suitable conclusion to the main part of the story.
6. On the basis of the ferryman's passengers, talk about the island community.
7. Discuss the author's use of names, and consider how these names contribute to the 'feel' or atmosphere of the story.
8. What actions or incidents in the story might stir in the reader (a) a sense of mystery, (b) a desire to laugh, (c) a feeling of disgust, (d) a sense of annoyance, and (e) a dislike of humanity?
9. Mirdale is mentioned first and last as well as in the middle of the story. Why is it so important in the ferryman's life?
10. Read again the first sentence and the last sentence; then consider what feelings towards the ferryman the author succeeds in arousing in his readers.

Clifford Hanley

SCHOOL DANCE

Nearly fifty years of life and nearly twenty-five years of marriage, and nothing to show for it except a houseful of people who had come from God knows where. Samuel Haddow often said the country was overrun with people.

It was a remark that had started as a fresh joke and flattened into a habit. There was a pair of socks in his chair, even.

'They're your own socks,' his wife told him, before he could complain. 'Peter hasn't got any black socks.'

'What do you mean, Peter hasn't got any black socks? Does he think he's taking these? He can go out and dirty a pair of white socks. My God, nothing's private.'

His son Peter stood in bare feet and underpants, with his back to the living-room fire and when Samuel glared at him, the boy shrugged his bony shoulders as if he was pleading innocence. Samuel didn't know whether this was more irritating than words. The boy seemed to have a genius for driving him over the edge of exasperation even by doing nothing at all.

'Oh, take the damn socks,' he muttered. What was so important about a pair of socks, that he should go mad over them? He had promised himself he would let it all flow over him and keep his temper. Fathers were supposed to be fond of their children, but a great deep well of irritation always opened up inside him as soon as he came home and found them there; especially Peter. The boy can't be as bad as that. I would give the damned socks away to a beggar and never miss them. But a beggar wouldn't take them for granted, that's the truth.

'You don't want him to look wrong when he's going to the school dance,' Mrs Haddow said apprehensively, trying to sound casual and businesslike. Her manner merely underlined her anxiety to avoid an outbreak of Samuel's temper, and this somehow irritated him even more.

'I said he could have the socks, I don't care about the socks, you're ironing that crease squinty.'

'Now you're not going to tell me how to press trousers after all these years,' Mrs Haddow said testily. 'Men don't know everything.'

'Here,' said Peter, 'I'll press the pants, and you can go and make the tea, Mum.'

'You'll press the pants!' Samuel's well of irritation bubbled again. 'You'll look sweet dancing wi' a hole the shape of an iron on your backside.'

'I'll be careful, Dad,' Peter said, quite reasonably.

'Aye, sure, you'll be careful.' Samuel forced himself to look at his evening paper. The boy *would* be careful, he wasn't in the habit of doing things badly. There was just something about the way he did them.

'I've got some nice spiced beef ham for your tea, Samuel,' his wife said brightly. Appeasing the monster. It was so transparent that a grin twitched at Samuel's mouth. What a bloody life. I'm a monster. Emily surrendered the iron to Peter reluctantly, convinced that he would ruin his good trousers. Men didn't have the touch for jobs like that.

But in the jumble of thoughts that lived in her head, she never lost sight of the need to take care of Samuel, even if Peter *did* arrive at the dance with his backside showing. Men were like babies, especially fathers, and it was important to let them see that they weren't being neglected in favour of their children. She had read it somewhere and its beautiful simplicity had startled her like a revelation of the Light.

The trousers were laid on a folded bedsheet on the living-room table, and Peter was pressing the iron on a damp cloth in a one-two, one-two-three rhythm and humming to himself. His feet began to twitch in sympathy. Samuel caught sight of them, past the edge of his newspaper, and grinned again. The boy was a bloody clown.

'You'd be better goin' in your bare feet,' he remarked. The derision in his voice was mere ingrained custom. 'Socks'll just hide that fancy toe stuff.'

'Yes, I do have rather pretty feet,' Peter said in a thoughtful, yah-yah voice, and Samuel looked to heaven and muttered, 'Oh God, he's got modesty like a wasting disease.' Julie, ten years old, came into the living-room, skinny and self-contained, and stared at Peter with a sneer.

'You look stupid,' she said. Peter answered with wolfish smile and laid his right foot flat against his left thigh.

It was always the same, there was always something going on, kids spilling over the whole house. Who were they? Christine, twenty, came home from work to find Peter dressed except for his shoes; wriggling the waistband of his trousers to try to make them hang lower. She swooped on him as if she had just created him and started tweaking his tie.

'Dere's a handsome wee brother,' she cooed. 'All nice and clean for his first dance.'

'Dere's a nice wee sister asking for a belt right in the chops,' Peter said. Samuel looked up sharply and then shrugged his shoulders.

'Who's taking you home tonight, Petesy-wetesy?' Christine asked. 'Whose heart is going to be broken?'

'Whose teeth are going to be broken in a minute?' Peter asked her, and she chuckled merrily.

'There, doesn't he look handsome, Mum?' Christine insisted. 'I think our wee Peter's too good for any of these schoolgirls.'

'Don't be silly, Christine,' Mrs Haddow said sharply. 'Peter's too young to be thinking about girls.'

'That's right, Mum—' Peter was saying patiently, when his father answered, 'He'll be dancin' wi' whippets.'

'—Corporation buses.' Peter finished, and his father grinned at him triumphantly. 'You're no' the only comic in the world,' he said. And Peter cried, 'Everybody gets inta de act!' Mrs Haddow looked vexed and uncomprehending, and Samuel and Peter exchanged a rare smile of collusion.

Peter insisted on leaving the house thirty minutes too early, choosing to walk the cold streets rather than suffer family fussing beyond the limits of endurance. He was unbearably embarrassed. There was frost on the ground.

His father said, 'Well, at least you look clean,' and turned back to his paper with the air of a man who is not going to be further bothered. When Peter had left, Samuel reflected sourly that he might have thought of giving the kid some money, his first school dance and everything. The omission nagged at him and spoiled his pleasure in his spiced beef ham.

Peter walked quickly and took deep breaths. The only light showing in the school came from a window of the janitor's house. The wooden gym annexe was in darkness. There would be red crêpe paper shrouding the white lamps. He had tied some of it on himself a few hours earlier. Six of them, the dance committee, had been excused the last two periods to get the gym ready. They had all been slightly hysterical, for no good reason. He thought back to try to savour the strange flavour of the afternoon.

Coming back from the gym they were all talking at once, and one of the girls slipped on the frozen path and fell into his arms and knocked him down, clutching him as they tumbled. As they lay absurdly on the path, laughing, he had had a sudden consciousness of the present, of living with unnatural vividness for a moment. The laughter, the crisp cold, the gathering darkness, the tingle of anticipation, glowed inside him.

During the last half-hour the dance started to lose its sense of confusion. Peter saw the gym clock showing a quarter to eleven and reminded himself that he was dancing with Honey and that he must be enjoying it. He stumbled and muttered sorry.

'My fault,' Honey said. 'You dance very well, for a school-kid.' Peter felt hot and pink, and ran his tongue across his front teeth to stop his lip from sticking on them.

'I should never have used that word,' he said. 'It gives you a weapon against me.'

'And don't I need it,' Honey muttered. 'You dance divinely, for a schoolteacher,' Peter said. Honey laughed and said, *'Touché.'* Peter tried to look casually round the gym. He couldn't pick out Lily anywhere.

'You're terribly beautiful, for a schoolteacher, too,' he said, and when Honey started to groan in protest, he went on, 'Well, you are, aren't you? You're much prettier than Mr Long.'

'As you were,' Honey said crisply. 'Don't start seducing me into disloyalty to the headmaster.' The word seduce hovered briefly in Peter's mind before he dismissed it. He gave up trying to pick out Lily in the crowd.

'It makes everything difficult,' he said, 'when you use your no-nonsense voice. It inhibits communication. What's the point of being a human being if human beings can't communicate with other human beings? Life becomes stale, flat, weary, and unprofitable.'

'Is this the way you frighten all the girls away?' Honey asked, and added hurriedly, 'I didn't mean that, it was just a joke. I find your conversation highly stimulating, Mr Haddow.'

'For a school-kid.' But they both smiled. The music stopped and Peter stepped back and bowed. Honey said, 'I can't tell you how much I've enjoyed dancing with you, Mr Haddow.'

'Try.'

'Oh, beat it,' Honey said, amused and exasperated. She dropped into a chair beside Gutty Greer and caught his eye.

'Kids,' she said, shaking her head. Peter overheard the word as he walked away, and smiled to himself. 'That Haddow's the worst,' Honey went on. 'He makes me feel like an old crone.'

'Astonishing, astonishing.' Gutty's thick lips barely moved, the sound came from somewhere in his chest.

'Where do they get the patter?' Honey wondered despairingly. 'Especially Haddow. Thank the Lord I'm stuck with first-year brats, I could never stand the pace with these adolescent wolves.'

'Glands, a matter of glands,' the words trickled out of the small space between Gutty's lips. 'You simply represent . . . um . . . a stimulus to the . . mm . . . endocrine system.'

'Why, Mr Greer,' said Honey, 'are you paying me a compliment?'

Anxious not to look anxious, Peter still couldn't see a trace of Lily. He couldn't see Big Joe Chadwick either. By the gym clock, there were ten minutes to go. What was the point in bothering? He had had the dance, and any minute people would start pouring into the cloakroom. There were some people there already. Peter backed casually towards the cloakroom to find his coat unobtrusively and disappear. One of the people already there was Jimmy Webster, whom Peter would fain have avoided.

'You chuckin' it as well?' Jimmy asked him; short, thin, and shrilly aggressive, ramming himself into his coat. 'Catch me gettin' lumbered, it's a mug's game.'

'Oh?'

'For God's sake!' Jimmy was vicious in his contempt. 'Walkin' two miles wi' some bird just for a cuddle.'

'It's a nice night for a walk,' Peter said blandly.

'With who?'

'Mind your own bee business,' Peter said amiably.

'Well, it's a funeral,' Jimmy said, toning down his derision. 'There's nothing in there that would keep *me* out of my bed.'

It would have been easy to make an unkind reply to Jimmy, but Peter felt sorry for him, and disliked him, and wished he would go away quickly. He did, and Peter watched him from the door until he left the playground and disappeared, walking with short, belligerent steps, before he himself left quickly in the opposite direction. There were three taxis at the school gate—for teachers, probably. Or could one be for Big Joe Chadwick? It was the kind of thing Big Joe could do, he always had money. Peter contemplated the idea of Big Joe in a taxi with Lily and found he could raise no emotion from it. This discovery irritated him slightly.

Big Joe was wearing a new suit tonight. He always had new suits. Peter looked down at his own feet. His trousers had crept up on him during the past months and no longer sat elegantly on his shoes. 'Durn you boy, your socks don't match,' he sang in an undertone. They did match.

He took the path across the waste ground, away from the housing scheme where he lived, and walked up and down streets to pass enough time to convince his sister Christine that he had taken a girl home, because Christine would be waiting at home for a cosy talk about it, and it never crossed his mind not to deceive her. The truth would only annoy her.

As he approached his house he saw two girls standing at the gate. One was Christine. With a small lifting of the spirits, Peter saw that the other was Jean Pynne.

'It's the conquering hero,' Christine said. 'This is my baby brother, Peter.'

'I know,' said Jean Pynne. She was probably the same age as Christine, about twenty. Seeing her seemed to diminish the importance of the dance. She was the legendary Jean Pynne, the fixed standard of comparison in all discussion on feminine beauty between Peter and his friends. She was dark and slender and gorgeous.

Christine tucked her arm into Peter's and leaned on him, and the display of sisterly warmth irritated him mildly because it seemed to signal the end of the conversation with Jean. She's only a girl, after all, Peter chid himself. But it wasn't true.

'Go on talking,' he said, and cleared his throat. 'Go on talking.'

'Come on, I want to hear everything about the Big Romance,' Christine said. Her air of self-conscious ownership was flattering but bothersome.

'There are some things a gentleman doesn't discuss,' he said, and Christine shook him impatiently. Jean Pynne said, 'Well, it's time I was away home. Cheerio.' She hung momentarily on her farewell. Just imagine, Peter thought, his mind racing. Just imagine taking Jean Pynne home. She's standing here talking to me—Jean Pynne. I'll never get the chance again.

'I'll walk you home.'

'What?' Christine was indignant. 'Two in the one night?'

'You must be freezing,' Jean said. It was mere politeness.

'Oh, I'm young and strong.'

'You're the limit,' Christine said. She was annoyed.

'I don't mind.' Jean Pynne laughed doubtfully, and Peter disengaged his arm from Christine's grasp.

'I'm not going to the moon,' he said. 'Women shouldn't be about at this time of the night without protection.'

'Ho, ho,' Christine scoffed. 'You get straight back here. I'm putting the kettle on now.' Peter fell into step beside Jean Pynne, wondering how it could have been so easy. They walked in silence, awkwardly, looking straight ahead.

'Did you enjoy the dance?' Jean asked him. Was there a hint of condescension in her voice? Peter shrugged.

'It was all right. Dancing is a rather lowbrow pastime, actually. I'm more of the intellectual type. You know, Hindu philosophy, all that trash.'

Jean gave a delicious little giggle. Her cheek was impossibly smoth and transparent and her teeth flashed white in the lamplight.

'You talk funny,' she said.

'It's because I'm adolescent,' Peter told her. 'I'm precociously immature. I talk too much. Sometimes I have to listen to myself making dopey jokes when I wish I would shut up or say something else. It's a disease.'

They walked on in silence.

'You see what I mean,' Peter said. 'The kind of things I say, nobody can say anything back. I bore me.'

'I don't mind.'

'You would if you were me.' This seemed funny, and he started to laugh. Jean laughed too, and a jolt of pure pleasure went through him at the sound, and at the prickling consciousness of her presence. It was mixed with a wild, terrible resentment that she couldn't realise how beautiful he found her; that telling her would merely sound like more words; and that her beauty could wring him while he had no effect on her at all.

'I mean,' he said, 'that in this situation I should start talking about the stars and the velvet curtain of the night, you know, that muck. For instance, the light from that star has taken two thousand years to reach us.'

'That makes me feel frightened,' Jean said, shuddering, and Peter instantly protested.

'Why? Stars are just bits of furniture, no matter how far away they are. It's human beings that matter. A hell of a lot of good it would do that starlight if it travelled for two thousand years and then we weren't here to see it. Don't let it browbeat you.' Jean laughed again, helplessly, and put one of her arms in his to support her. Peter squeezed tight on it and imprisoned it as they walked on.

'How did you ever get home?' Jean asked him, '—if you've been talking like this to somebody else?'

'Can I talk seriously to you?'

'If you like.'

'I didn't see any girl home from the school dance. I didn't have the nerve. I talk a lot, but I'm a coward.'

'That's a shame,' said Jean. 'Imagine how the girls feel that nobody took home. It's awful, you don't know how awful it is.'

This novel view of the situation startled Peter, who had hoped for warm sympathy.

'I didn't think of that,' he admitted. 'I suppose I'm a rat, as well as a coward.'

'I would probably be just as bad, if I was a boy,' Jean said.

'Ah, it's a terrible business, sex,' Peter said, and added, 'I don't mean sex, like that. I mean, having two sexes in the world. It truly baffles me. I bet you're fed up listening to me.'

'No, honestly, don't be silly.'

'Well, half the people are one sex and half the people are the other sex. *All the time,* I mean. When you think of all the trouble it causes. What if everybody was the same sex most of the time, and then just a different sex occasionally, or if there was no sex most of the time and just sex now and then, like dressing up for Hallowe'en. Do you know this? I've started to talk absolute nonsense again.'

'I don't quite get it.'

'Good. I don't either. But it truly baffles me anyway. How do I *know* some girl wanted me to take her home from the dance? If some girl did. There should be some better system. I don't even know what to say to a girl. I talk a lot, but I don't know. I don't know what they're thinking.'

'They're just ordinary, they just think ordinary things.'

Peter gave a short, bitter laugh.

'All right,' he said, 'say I had taken some girl home from the dance—'

'What's her name?'

'She hasn't got a name,' he blustered. 'It's just a hypothesis. So I take her home. I still don't know what she's thinking, and she doesn't know what I'm thinking. Does she want me to kiss her good night? The way we talk in the class, we're all big guys, men of the world, we've done everything, but that's what it boils down to, does this girl want us to kiss her good night? And how do you start?'

'I don't know,' Jean said helplessly. 'It's up to the boy.'

'Well, do I break off in the middle of a sentence about trigonometry and woof! Probably land in her eye, or her ear,' he added glumly.

'It can't be as difficult as that, if she likes you. It shouldn't be difficult for you, anyway. Most of the boys that used to take me home couldn't say anything at all, and neither could I. You can talk.'

Peter brightened at once. 'Could I have talked you into kissing me good night—if I was taking you home from a dance?'

'What is this leading up to?' Jean looked sideways at him and saw him shake his head and saw his bony baffled face and felt that she had been elected to the status of a woman of the world. How old was Peter? And how was a sophisticate supposed to act in this situation? They had reached her gate, and Peter still had her arm in his.

'There's nothing to it,' Jean said shakily. She raised her free arm to touch his cheek and turn his face towards her, and kissed him lightly on the mouth. 'See?'

'Hey,' Peter said. 'You kissed me.'

Jean disengaged her arm firmly.

'It was just a demonstration.' She opened the gate and

moved to the inside of it. 'Now you'll know next time.' She giggled in spite of her determination to be calm and controlled. Peter was standing with his arms hanging limply by his sides.

'Well, good night,' he said. Jean ran up to the front door, but he called after her, and she turned round.

'Thank you!' he called in a whisper. Jean waved her arm and vanished into the house. Inside the front door she stopped to find that she was blushing and breathless. Soft as a jelly, she accused herself in irritation. For God's sake, I'm nineteen.

Peter walked home briskly, looking thoughtful, and now and then gravely jumping sideways to kick his heels together. He went in by the back door to find Christine in the kitchen making a fine show of annoyance.

'This dancing's gone to your noddle, my boy,' she chid him. 'Just who the blazes do you think you are, Casanova?'

'Can I help it if I'm rugged and handsome and irresistible to women?'

'You conceited little pig,' said Christine, ramming an Abernethy biscuit into his mouth while he grinned vacuously without resisting. 'That's the last time this kid waits up to make your supper. Well, what was the dance like?'

'It was all right,' he said.

'How was your dancing? I hope you relaxed, for God's sake.' Peter waved a dismissal of such trivialities. 'Nothing to it,' he sprayed.

' "Nothing to it," he says. God, my aching feet after the way I shoved you round the living-room floor. How did David do?'

'David did all right,' said Peter, in world-weary tones. 'For a Clydesdale. I know you think Davie's a sweety-pie, but he's no advertisement for your training. He'll never dance like your brother. Earnest but clueless, that's our Davie.'

Christine was determined to wring everything from him.

'Did you take somebody home? Who was it, after all? Lily?'

'What do you know about Lily?'

'Oh, give us strength. You've had Lily coming out of your ears for weeks, whoever she is. Even David thinks you're daft about her.'

'My pal Davie,' Peter said bitterly, 'And his big Severn-tunnel gub. All right, I took Lily home. A nice wee thing, but immature, immature.'

'Don't come the big-man stuff here,' Christine crushed him. 'Just because you walked Jean Pynne round the block.'

'Jean's nice,' Peter said thoughtfully, and Christine threw another biscuit at him, crying, 'She's out of your class, infant!' She would have said more, but Peter fielded the biscuit and threw it back, and Christine had a fit of the giggles. Peter went to bed and lay on his back with his eyes open.

GLOSSARY

squinty: askew, awry

belt right in the chops: blow on the mouth

patter: smart talk

chuckin' it: giving it up

lumbered: burdened

Hallowe'en: All-hallows Eve when children in Scotland dress up in strange, outlandish costumes

TALKING POINTS

1. The first part of the story takes place at home, and introduces us to Peter's parents and sisters. What aspects of family relationships are revealed here, and how does the author succeed in making his account of family life entertaining?
2. Read again the two paragraphs of interlude—between the first scene at home and the second scene at the

dance—that describe Peter's thoughts as he walks 'the cold streets'. What do we learn here about his mood or feelings before the dance?

3. A highlight of the evening for Peter comes in the last half-hour of the dance when he finds himself dancing with Honey. What does the witty conversation tell us (a) about Honey, (b) about Peter, and (c) about their opinion of each other?
4. After the dance there comes another interlude for Peter when he is obliged to walk home by himself. What would you say was his mood at this point? What do you think lies behind his thoughts about Big Joe and Lily?
5. The walk home with Jean Pynne becomes for Peter the climax of the evening. Consider the change that comes over his conversation. What is the effect of the kiss (a) on Peter, and (b) on Jean herself? In what sense is this episode a turning-point in Peter's life?
6. Consider how far the last scene at home with Christine is necessary for rounding off the story. Read again the last passage of dialogue; then discuss Peter's attitude to Christine's questioning, and say which words you think best reveal the change that has come over him.
7. What might be the overall meaning of the last four words of the story?
8. Peter is the central figure or hero. How does the author convey to us that he is (a) bright, (b) at an awkward age, (c) a member of a closely-knit family, and (d) really insecure and uncertain of himself?
9. In many short stories the 'hero' is engaged in some battle with life. What are the little battles Peter engages in, and what is his greatest battle?
10. 'I talk a lot but I'm a coward.'
    This could be regarded as the real theme of the story. What was Peter afraid of? How was the fear banished once and for all?

Naomi Mitchison

ON AN ISLAND

By morning it was worse Kenny was. She herself had dozed off for maybe an hour, between black night and the time when the lamp by the window began to look queer. The fire was down, but when she blew on it the peats flared again. The kettle would be boiling in a wee while. He would like a cup tea surely. Nothing to eat, the doctor had said. But how then would he keep his strength up? Maybe an egg—. From where she was by the fire she kept on looking back over her shoulder at him on the bed, not himself at all, a stranger in their own bed, in Kenny's body, pulling at the red blankets.

She made the tea, strong, with plenty of sugar, the way Kenny liked it. But the stranger pushed it away. She hardly knew whether to speak to him in the English or the Gaelic. But he answered to neither.

She looked out; it was low tide. The doctor would cross the ford easy. She had better see to the cow and the hens before he would be coming. Her mother came up past the back of the dyke. She looked at the stranger in the bed, and shook her head.

'Go you to the cow, Beitidh,' she said. 'I will sit with him. Will he not take his tea? Well, well. But it is a pity to waste a good cup.'

After she had fed the hens, Beitidh came back with the milk pail and set the half of it for cream.

'I will churn Saturday,' she said. 'He will be better then.'

For indeed it was a bonny fresh morning and she felt better herself, and that way she had a certainty that he too would be better. But her mother, sitting ben by the bed, gave her a look that spoilt that, and oh, now it came to her that Kenny would never dig his knife into the golden butter never again, and she sat down on the wee stool by the window and put her head down in her hands, and she had cried the edge of her skirt wet through by the time she heard the doctor's car.

He did not speak much to her, only made her hold the lamp near, for it was kind of dark over by the bed. He was listening and feeling about, and Kenny began to moan, to make noises not like himself, not like Kenny, who was so strong and clever, and her hand shook, holding the lamp, and her mother's eyes on her were sorrowful and certain.

The doctor was speaking and at first she had trouble understanding him.

'But we havena been in an aeroplane, neither of the two of us,' she said. 'He would know——'

'He will not need to know,' said the doctor. 'And all you need to do yourself is to wrap him up warm. I will be with him to the hospital.'

'But—but then—how will I know?'

'You will just go over with Donny's van to Stronbost and you will get Mrs Morrison at the Post Office to ring up the hospital,' he looked at his watch, 'round about four o'clock, and you will know then.'

'Och, I'm no' just sure—if I want him to go at all, Doctor—not so far—I will need to think it over!'

'Beitidh,' said the doctor, 'there is no time for thinking it over. The 'plane is on its way from Renfrew. Give me some safety pins now and we will wrap him up.'

She felt in the drawer for them blindly. He was taking Kenny away, she had no power to stop him. And what would they do with him at the hospital—och, she would never see him again!

The 'plane came down on the sand, and then, before she was used to it at all, the doctor and a strange kind of nurse had bundled Kenny in, with red blankets round him, and he not saying good-bye, not knowing even they had taken him away. The door shut on her, and the thing left in a terrible wind and noise, and it was as though part of herself had been pulled away with it.

Her mother had everything straightened up within, and the bed made again, with her other blankets, the old plain ones that she used to sleep under before ever she was married on Kenny.

'If it is the Lord's will,' said her mother, 'we must not be the ones to complain. And maybe it is as well now that you have no bairns. For you will marry again, surely.'

Soon her sister came in and two more of the neighbours, and they put on the kettle again. 'Och, well, well, poor Kenny,' they were saying. 'He was a good lad. It was a terrible pity for him to be going this way.'

And she sat, half listening while they spoke of one or another who had died, either at home or after being taken away to the hospital. And the thing beat on her and now all the months of her life with Kenny had gone small and far. And she began looking ahead, past the things that were to be done. For they would bring back the corpse from the hospital as it had been done before with others. It would come by the boat, and they would go down to meet it. She would need to go to the store for a black dress; she had the coat. There was money saved enough for everything. All of a sudden she saw Kenny's hand putting the silver money into the jug at the back of the press, Kenny's own strong hand, and she burst out weeping and ran from the house. The rest looked on her with compassion and fell again to speaking of the ways of death.

Donny's van was on the far side of the flood, and the boat would be crossing, for it was high tide now. She took her place in the bows; she must carry out the things the doctor had told her; she must receive the news. Old Hamish had a web of tweed to ferry across, but he put it and himself in the stern of the boat and was joined by two of the crofters. They spoke in low voices, aware of her alone in the bows.

She climbed into the van and the road went by and the dark banks of peat and the dark shining water over the peat, and they came into the long scatter of houses that was Stronbost, a few black houses still, like their own, but mostly the new concrete ones. There had been a time when she and Kenny had spoken together of how they would build themselves a white house with a good chimney and maybe a bathroom later on, and he would get the grant from the Board. And that seemed all terrible long ago now.

She went into the store, and whispered to Mrs Morrison how she needed to telephone to the hospital, and could it be done. Mrs Morrison said it was the easiest thing in the world and brought her to the telephone and spoke into the thing, and there was clicking and slamming and then it was the hospital, and oh, it was beyond her altogether to speak into it herself, to ask the question and to get the answer! But Mrs Morrison was brisk, she spoke, she asked. 'Here is the doctor now,' she said. 'Speak you, Betidh.' And then calling into the black mouth of the telephone, 'This is Beitidh here, Doctor.'

'He has been through the operation,' the doctor said, 'and he is getting on fine.'

'Oh, Doctor, Doctor!' said Beitidh into the thing, 'is it living he is? Is it living, my Kenny?'

'Aye,' said the doctor. 'Just that. We were in time.'

'Och,' said Beitidh. 'I thought—I thought—'

And then she began to laugh like a daft thing, and the black mouth of the telephone grinned at her, the way it could have been laughing too.

GLOSSARY

ben: inside, within

press: cupboard

the Board: a government agency operating in the highlands.

TALKING POINTS

1. Read the first two paragraphs again; then discuss the thoughts that pass through the mind of the young wife as she tends her sick husband, and the various feelings she must be experiencing.
2. Compare the attitude of the mother towards the sick man with the attitude of Beitidh herself. What effect does the mother's attitude have on Beitidh?
3. What does the talk between Beitidh and the doctor bring out (a) about the doctor, and (b) about Beitidh? What attitudes show Beitidh to be a simple or uncomplicated kind of woman?
4. What does everyone assume is to happen to Kenny at the hospital? Consider the effect of the conversation of the mother and the sister on Beitidh. What is it that causes her to break down?
5. The final scene takes place in Mrs Morrison's store at Stronbost. How does the author show that Beitidh is not accustomed to the telephone? What would you say was the climax or turning-point of the story?
6. There are two references to the 'black mouth of the telephone' separated by Beitidh's talk with the doctor and her laughing. Why do you think she laughed? What suggests her attitude to the telephone has changed by the end of the story?
7. Do you think Beitidh would be the same woman after her experience? Say in what ways you think she might be different.
8. Consider the title of the story. In what sense, apart from being an inhabitant, can the main character be said by her situation to be 'on an island?'
9. From the special words and turns of phrase used, what kind of person does the author pretend to be for the purpose of telling the story?

10. The story is told almost entirely from the point of view of the young wife, and yet it is not told in the first person. In what ways does this method of story-telling help to make the story more vivid and more interesting to us as listeners or readers?

Appendix

MAKING A SHORT STORY

One of the most interesting ways of learning to use language effectively is to employ it in the telling of a story. Human beings of all ages and in all countries are interested in the happenings or situations in the world around them, as we can see from newspapers, radio and television, or from the question we are always hearing —'What happened today?'

The making of a short story involves much more than a bald account of a series of events, even though some such account may be the basis or starting point of a short story in the writer's mind. We have to be selective. If we are going to write the normal kind of short story, we are going to concern ourselves with only a few human beings and with only a few of the actions they perform at certain times in their lives. We shall be dealing with only a few of the words they say to each other, with only a few of the things they think and feel, and with only one or two places at which they perform their actions. Let us consider the kind of opportunities this selection and these elements give us to write interesting stories.

First of all let us think of the people, or characters as they are called, in our story. As we have said, the number of these should be limited; but if we choose just one there will be difficulty in making a story that has much point. Of these there should be one who is the central character—or perhaps two who are of equal status, the others being important only for the effect they have on the central character or characters.

In the choice of actors in your little drama of life you may want to consider (a) their ages—from the very young to the very old, (b) their place in society—from tramps to kings, (c) their nationality or the district or town from which they come, (d) their special traits of character, (e) whether they are male or female, (f) their names or whether they are to remain anonymous, (g) their appearance, and (h) their occupation.

As a short story has to show people in action, we have to have incidents or a plot of some kind, some sequence of events, each separate part of which leads on eventually to a significant happening in the life of the main character. There are roughly three main kinds of story pattern. The first is that in which events are arranged in a strictly chronological order and built up to a climax near the end; the second is that in which the writer begins part of the way through the story, then 'flashes back' or reveals what led up to this point, before going on to his climax; the third is that in which some weakness or flaw or obsession is revealed at work in a series of impressions or situations. Usually, in all three types of story, the central character should have some kind of significant experience that alters his life or his attitude towards living.

A good pattern for beginners is to have an opening situation, in which the main character has a problem, followed by a series of little episodes in which he is more and more troubled, and ending with the climax or crisis in which he has to take a decision or undergo an important experience. The new pattern or way of living that results can be briefly stated or suggested in the dénouement. Usually a short story is more effective if we can concentrate all the events into a short space of time.

When we are thinking of the kind of incidents to select, we must remember there is a wide variety in type and quality to choose from. We may use happenings that are funny, odd, grotesque, horrible, romantic, tender, brutal, disgusting, happy, sad.

It is not absolutely necessary that we should make our characters live and move in some definite place or places—we can have them merely talk and do things; but it is normal to make clear to our readers just where the events are taking place. By describing the setting or background we can give realism to the story or we can create an atmosphere. Or we can add interest, for we have the whole world to choose from, by placing the story in an unusual region or country. Of course, we must decide how much description of background we think necessary for our story and just where we want to introduce such descriptions. Two particular places in the story at which the setting may be described are first in the opening and secondly, to create suspense, before an important action. If we like, we can do what film makers do—include background to show its effect on a character's feelings or state of mind or action. But as a short story is mostly concerned with human beings in action, we should guard against overloading our story with pure description.

A story without dialogue or speech is liable to be dull, because speech is the most characteristic of human activities and the one most indulged in. Our short story will be more natural and convincing if characters are made to speak instead of being made only to go through motions like dummies. Speech, by its own kind of language, can show a person's position in the social scale, his place of origin, his educational background. It can also suggest qualities of character and emotional states or moods; and it can be effectively used at tense or dramatic moments in a narrative. To use dialogue properly, however, we have to be quite sure of the rules of punctuation for direct speech.

One of the most important aspects of story-telling or short-story writing concerns the method of narration. Three common methods are available to us. In the first we may choose to tell a story in the first person, as ourselves, from within, as if we were present at every incident and were telling what was passing before our very eyes. In the second we may choose to use the third person and write as if we were outside the story but were all-knowing about the characters and circumstances. In the third we may choose what is known as a 'persona', that is someone different from ourselves. For example, a man may choose to tell the story as a woman or a girl; or a woman may choose to tell the story as a journalist, as a sympathetic friend, as a hostile neighbour, as a six-year-old boy. If we choose a persona we should try to maintain the character and characteristics of that person throughout.

Connected with the method of narration is the tone or angle we decide to adopt. The same story can be told by people of widely different attitudes and points of view. Hence we should know whether we want to tell it as bitter critics of humanity, as lovers of mankind, as romantics, as realists, as humorists or wits, as angry young men or women, and so on. Adopting a definite point of view increases the originality of the story and its interest.

When we are young and still at school, we may not see so keenly into the complexities of life that we can make a story with a deep theme, that is one that makes a comment on the nature of our existence here in the world. Yet, as young people, we may want to write stories that reflect opinions on, for example, race relations, cruelty to animals, vandalism, drug taking, or any other social problem.

Good short stories are not written by accident. When you next come to attempt one we hope you will plan it in the light of some of the hints and suggestions we have made, and in the light of what you have learned from reading the stories in this volume.

R.M.
J.T.L.

Acknowledgements

The editors and publishers wish to thank the following for permission to use copyright material: Mr Alexander Reid for *A Warm Golden Brown*; William Blackwood & Sons Ltd for *The Small Herdsman* by Eona Macnicol from *Hallowe'en Hero and Other Stories*; Mr J. F. Hendry for *The Disinherited*; Methuen & Co Ltd for *Alicky's Watch* from *The Last Sister* by Fred Urquhart; Victor Gollancz Ltd for *The Telegram* from *The Black and the Red* by Iain Crichton Smith; Mr J. T. Low for *Jemima*; The Hogarth Press for *The Ferryman* from *A Calendar of Love* by George Mackay Brown; Hutchinson Publishing Group for *School Dance* from *A Taste of Too Much* by Clifford Hanley; Allen & Unwin for *On an Island* from *Five Men and a Swan* by Naomi Mitchison. *Murdoch's Bull* by Edward Scouller first appeared in *The Modern Scot*, ed. Fred Urquhart.